DARK FEATHER

ANNA BONDE HINKE

America Star Books
Frederick, Maryland

First printing

All characters in this book are fictitious, and any resemblance to real persons, living or dead, is coincidental.

America Star Books has allowed this work to remain exactly as the author intended, verbatim, without editorial input.

Softcover 9781634480420
PUBLISHED BY AMERICA STAR BOOKS, LLLP
www.americastarbooks.com
Frederick, Maryland

PROLOGUE

Darkness; a burning kind of dark. That was all I could feel - the darkness climbed in everywhere, darkness pressing against my eyes, my hands bound by thick ropes of dark, and I could hear someone screaming, could hear their desperate cries for help. Perhaps it was just me, alone, in the middle of the darkness. Alone. The first tear fell.

Dark.
Tear.
Fight.
Dark.
Teardrop.
Fuck.
Save me.

Chapter One

It was a cool evening in the fall - end of September, to be exact - the day my life changed forever. I don't know any other way to put it, even though that is such an overused sentence. I can remember that day very vividly, and not just because of all the things that happened afterwards. The evening burned itself just in the retina of my eyes - they are blue, by the way. My mother used to say that they were blue as the sea, that I was a 'sea-daughter'. I 'belonged to the sea' or whatever. Sounded like they'd tried to drown me as a baby.

In my opinion, it was rather macabre... But maybe there was something about all the nonsense about me belonging to the sea - it was there I was, on that night; at the harbor, anyway, if you want to call that the ocean. There was no wild nature here. The closest thing this place came to nature were the weeds that grew up between the cobbles. I had been walking around the little town, and had ended up sitting there, on a stone.

I'd read a good deal of books in my fifteen year long life – not an overwhelming lot of them, (never enough in my opinion, actually), but enough to know, that the main character always know when something in their lives is about to change drastically – either that, or they're completely oblivious.

I was supposed to have picked up on the little things, but I ended up completely oblivious in the harbor at around nine in the evening, and hadn't fit the puzzle pieces together. It was typical for me, really; I was the kind of girl that stumbled through life, never really knowing who the people around her was, never really recognizing the places she saw, and never really knowing who she herself was. I was an in-between; someone in the crowd, especially in school. There I wasn't really a nerd, but not really the troublemaker either, although I'd been sent to principal's office a couple times; not really liked, but not hated either. I was just a part of the wallpaper in my school. Nothing but plain, white and boring.

It had, in fact, been my last day of school that day - it was the intention that I was to start in a new school on the following Monday. I supposed that the idea behind the transfer were to give me friends; the fact that I hadn't brought any friends home since third grade - I didn't really have any friends; at least not in school, weighed my parents down. My best friend was my three year younger cousin. The only thing I really would be sad to leave at school was Louisa. It wasn't even because we were friends - far from it. The closest we came in contact was to stand behind each other in Physical Education.

And that – that was one of the signs I should have noticed. I had been stood before her in a row in P.E. that day, and she had poked me on the shoulder and with a slight laughter greeted me. It was the first, and the only sign I should've needed. That laughter, and that poke. That poke and that laughter. Louisa.

The second sign – if you even could call an emotion a sign - was my instinctive urge to go down to the harbor. I was watching TV in the evening as always, watching one of my favorite shows, a comedy, (that, as legend had it, once should've been about talent for singing) just had ended, closing credits running down the screen, while I was sitting there in my mother's soft sofa, and I knew it. I knew that I had to get some air, and I had to get it now; I grabbed a random sweater, and I had in my hurry taken two different colored sneakers, a black and a green; but in the end I managed to finally to lock me out of our house I lived in with mom. My dad left when I was seven years old. They got divorced and he moved to New York. I rarely ever saw him.

There was no 'third sign'. My life was, and is, no fairytale.

I had been in the process of balancing on the edge of the paving stones close to the water - when I saw it. It was something like a floating light. I say 'floating', because I don't know how I'm supposed to describe it; it was a small ball of light - it was light right? - nearly on the water surface, and almost swam toward me. For one reason or another I shut my eyes tightly; perhaps I knew at that moment that my life would change completely, perhaps I was trying to escape before that change happened. Everything went a little too quickly, and I thought I would fall to the ground if things were to keep happening at that pace. Things were spinning a little – I didn't know what to do… I was going to count to 10 inside, with my eyes closed. Count to 10, and when you open your eyes, everything will be normal again. Did I even want that at all, everything to be normal?

One. What was that sound? Three. 's it waves? Four. Shouldn't I open my eyes? 5. I'm going to open my eyes. Now. I forced my eyes open, and pushed my brown fringe out of my eyes.

In front of me was a girl. She could not be much older than me - maybe by a year or two. The first that struck me about her was that she was naked, completely and utterly naked, as if she had just been born, no more than a thought until the moment she was in front of me. Quite bold of her to swim in the harbor, naked even. Probably quite dangerous to swim in there in this weather. She would certainly get an inflammation of the cold. I would not have dared to do so myself.

Her hair was light - jaw-dropping light, bright as on a small child in summer, even though she had just been in the water; and, in front of my eyes, the color changed; now it was more blonde than white; then more a light brown than blond, until she was left, with the light brown hair flowing a little bit in the fall breeze. I had a feeling that I would have to be able to see her hair grow in the moments which had gone while my eyes had been closed. As in the first of the stories about Narnia where you could see the trees grow - Polly and Digory had entered in another world which was created by pure tones, song; music.

Her skin was pale, and trembling with goose bumps - her breasts distended; her whole body shivering. Each hair stood up on her pale skin, as she with unsteady hands raised an arm to wave to someone.

There was no one but me, but yet I still pointed to myself and mimed, "me?"

She did not reply; in fact she didn't really do anything, other than stepping closer to me and waved again, her entire palm spread out along with all her five fingers – I'd been expecting some kind of alien hand, but it seemed perfectly normal, maybe a little blue from the cold, as she continued waving, back and forth, back and forth.

"Are you some kind of alien to teach me about Cosmos and Chaos?" I asked, and remembered in a glimpse a book I had read when I was a kid; a little boy had met an alien, whom had made him question everything about his existence.

"An ali - Wha', an alien? No, I am not an alien, if you mean a 'weird-green-thing-from-Mars'-kind-of-alien," she replied, and smiled at me with a slight laughter. Her teeth, that I unconsciously had expected was just like a celebrity - perfectly straight and white; was a little crooked, like a person who really should use braces. That reassured me in a special way. I had not noticed that my heart beat several times as fast as it should, before I felt it slow down. .

Perhaps that was the moment I realized what I had said – what I had asked.

I had asked a girl if she was an alien - an alien. A naked girl. I shook my head apologetically, and shrugged lightly at her.

"Amy, you." she said, with her quirky, far from perfect, smile, and held out a hand toward me - I was not sure whether she asked for my name, or commanded me to say it. For one reason or another I felt as if I wouldn't have been offended even if she'd done the latter.

"Emma," I said and gave her hand - and in the moment I did, the memory of Louisa who had poked me on the shoulder came into my head, and I thought that I ought to have realized that it meant something very special... and then there were space for a second image in my head; I stood in front the class and gave everyone small cream puffs out as my way of saying goodbye to the class, and Louisa sat on a seat that actually belonged to Kylee P. as she - Louisa – didn't even have this class, and really shouldn't be there. It had given me a strange feeling inside ... her eyes had seen disappointed into mine, with the gray-blue color her eyes have, the eyelashes weighed down with a layer of mascara. She had said no thanks to the puff which I technically shouldn't be offering her since she technically shouldn't be there ... but I didn't care about all the technical problems of Louisa sat on the place.

That look had burned itself into my retina once again- and that was why this day was a special day.

That momentary doubt of whet ether it was a good idea to start all over again somewhere new; that was why this day was special.

Amy tilted her head.

"Can I borrow some clothes, Emma?" she asked, as if she understood that I was buried deeply in thought; "you were thinking of something important, I could see it in your eyes," she said, while I took action and gave her the sweater I had been wearing; she tried to pull down to cover her private parts, obviously having quite the problem with the not very covering outfit, but not saying anything. We just stood there, and looked confused – at least I think that was what we felt - at each other a moment, before she reached out a hand, and said, with a gentle voice,

"Come," while she, with the other hand, tugged at the sweater to cover herself up. When I received her hand it struck me what was special about this; it felt strangely intimate, a little bit too much; the straw that broke the camel's back.

And there was also something else that felt... strange.

"Should I know you, Amy?" I asked, as I ran a few steps to keep up with her, clenching her hand in my own, trying to get her nails to scrape against my palm. Was this a dream? Would I wake up in a few minutes time, continuing my life like nothing had happened – because genuinely, nothing had happened.

"Yes," she replied. And then we went there, walking on the cobbles.

CHAPTER TWO

It was strange to walk there along with Amy, to hold her hand and feel so completely free. I didn't exactly know a lot about friendship - my best (and only) friend was my cousin Annabelle. She was three years younger than me, and still insisted to jump on a trampoline whenever we met up at her house. This was completely different than holding onto her hand while we hopped off as loudly as we could, or singing at the top of our lungs. I realized how lonely I actually felt over only hanging out with Annabelle, even if she was my best friend, and even if we had the same blood running through our veins – some days it just wasn't enough to have Annabelle. Some days I just missed having other friends, even if I didn't know what to do with that, even if I didn't know how to be the friend that other people wanted, simply because Annabelle was the only person willing to be; some days I just wanted other friends so desperately that I'd do anything to feel accepted. It felt like I was going crazy sometimes. It felt like my family had set me up for breeding, like an animal, and the only one they wanted to pair me with was my own cousin.

Some days I was willing to follow a stranger, just because it felt right to do so. Some days I was willing to quit the world just because the world always was ready to quit me, like the stub from a cigarette on the street – no one noticed it as anything. No one noticed it. Some days I felt like a cigarette stub beneath a shoe, beneath the weight of life.

As I walked there, balancing on the cobbles once again, the mysterious girl tugging a little bit at me as we walked, her in front of me, dragging me along, it felt like an entire new world had been born, and I was walking in the middle of it. That was really the only way I could describe it – it was all so new, strange and mysterious… so different from Annabelle and her trampoline… and scarier; so incredibly scary.

"Do you know what your name means?" she asked, turning her head to look at me, as she tried to gracefully (read: clumsily tried to) step over a bump of stones. I shook my head, and followed her example. She continued talking, not giving the stone she'd been tripping over a single glance back; "I don't want to sound like an alien or whatever you think I am – but how can you know who you are, if you don't even know what your name means, Emma?"

I was glad she couldn't see my face at the moment – it gave me the ability to think the question over. Did I know who I was? Did anyone even know who they were? Her thumb caressed mine lightly, calmingly. How strange wasn't it – how I entire life had tried to figure out who I was, and then she came along, and asked me just that question, just to pour salt in the open wound. Nobody, least of all me, knew who I was. Nobody knew what my dreams or hopes were; nobody knew my personality – if I even had one. I was one with the plain wallpaper. I was wallpaper. Just as insignificant as the plain, white, boring wallpaper. I was Boring Emma.

Out of a sudden she stopped walking. She released my hand and tugged at the sweater again, before she sat down on the edge, close to the water. It looked dark, like oil; like it'd drag you down and eat you up, swallowing one's soul, devouring you completely. Down and down and down I'd go, into a vortex, if I fell down there.

"How can you know, Emma? How can you know who you are?" she asked, and reached out for my hand with an imperfect, crooked smile and a dimple in the cheek, that reminded me of someone else that I just couldn't allow myself to think of, and that -

That was when I snapped. I couldn't help it – it was like a cartoon where somebody showed the bull the red napkin and it started running. I screeched out the words in anger, as the fuming fifteen-year old I was;

"No, okay, stop, this is freaking me out, Amy, whoever – whatever you are, stop it. I'm done, I'm going home, I- fucking freak! You're – you're psycho. My parents taught me not to speak to strangers!"

I turned my back onto her a second too late – I saw the way her eyebrows raised in confusion and then fell again, just like her entire face fell a little. I saw the disappointment in her eyes; I saw how her lips drooped a little, and her dimple disappeared, as she sighed deeply. It was like her entire being faded a little bit, like a paper filled with words left in the rain. She looked smudged and dirty, like snow in spring – except there were no beautiful trees blooming in beauty waiting for the snow to disappear. It was snow falling too early on the year, melting already, dirty and unwanted in the mud. My vision got blurry, my eyelashes getting stuck on my skin, my hair flapping against my cheeks as I shook my head again – and once more, as I started to walk back home.

A droplet hit the ground. Was that tears? Was I crying? I didn't want to be crying. Crying was stupid. Weak, even. I dried my cheeks, and sniffled lightly. I was not crying.

When another droplet fell, crashing onto the paving stones, I dared to look up. The clouds were dangerously dark. Run. I ran. And I was definitely not crying.

The words echoed frighteningly in my head, stopped making sense, got scrambled together, and mixed up themselves up with one another.

How can you know who you are who you are you are are. How can you know you know you know who you are? Emma, how can you know?

I ran almost the whole way home, looking down on the ground every second of it; I made sure that I stepped on each cigarette stub I saw, as I ran until my legs were sore and my feet burned, and even beyond that; my lungs felt like they had punctuated by the time I finally did a halt, tried to even out my breath, calm my heartbeat. I waited for the world to stop spinning, then I collected myself – it felt like I had been turned inside out, heart, liver, and organs pouring out of me as well as all my emotions, all the sudden sorrow and anger, and I had to pick up the pieces and continue to walk on. How are you supposed to collect yourself when you don't know who you're supposed to be?

Maybe I lost a part of myself there, on the street. That would've explained why I felt so down, that would've explained why I didn't know if I was crying or if the droplets on my face were from rain... That would've explained me lashing out at my mom the moment the front door was shut. It wouldn't have justified it, but it would've explained it. It would've explained how I slammed the front door before mom had arrived in the doorway to the kitchen to greet me with an earful about the fact that I had just left, without telling her. It would've explained how, and why, I started to cry, the tears pouring out of my eyes, in the very second I saw my mom standing in front of me – Mom, with her perfect page hair-cut and perfect makeup. I couldn't help but cry. I didn't want to be crying, but I was definitely doing just that –the tears falling quickly and never ending.

"What happened?" It wasn't even a question; it was a command. My mom was demanding to know what had happened. I raised my middle finger in the sky as I slid through the door to my own room, slamming the door after me, searching for the key, and locked it, before I broke down in tears again.

She was screeching like a crow outside of my door, just like I had screeched at that girl earlier... "Emma, what happened? Emma?" Frantic knocking on my door, again and again, again and again. My body felt numb, as I found myself my most comfy pullover and dragged up the hood. I felt so incredibly numb – I was nothing but a cigarette stub beneath a shoe.

The reflection of my face looked pale as a bone as I looked out of the window, searching for enemies in the busy street lights, watching the never sleeping city. Pacing scared back and forth in my room, because Idon'tunderstandIdon'tunderstandIdon'tu nderstand, and because I had a feeling that I'd never understand what was going on right now... It scared me. I plugged in my headphones, and sat down on the windowsill.

I sat there for hours, looking out of the window, almost waiting for the mysterious girl to show up again. I sat there for hours, with my headphones in, watching the cars drive by, and wondered if She was sitting in one of them. I sat there for hours, listening to the music that created other worlds. I sat there for hours, waiting and watching.

Maybe I was even looking for that missing piece of me driving by in one of those cars.

CHAPTER THREE

Monday morning hit me in the face like a solid brick wall, when the all too familiar tune of my alarm clock started playing.

Truth to be told, I had spent most of the weekend moping over the change from one crappy public school to another, just as crappy public school. I knew one of my teachers would be one of my mom's friends, Mrs. SoCreepy or something. Of course I had the cliché talks with Annabelle over the phone on Saturday night, talking about how we'd always stick together... But we both knew that our friendship was hanging in a thread thin enough already and that risking our friendship was dangerous enough – it was definitely not possible for us to meet as often as we had used to -; it was already guaranteed that it would be put to the test...

I just had to stop myself from ruining the remains of our friendship... especially because of the fact that we'd never be free from each other. We'd have to face one another again and again, simply because we had the same blood running in our veins – even on the off change I'd get friends on my own in this new school, I'd be stuck with Annabelle forever, even if I didn't want to. That was something I thought a lot about, especially after that night on the harbor, even though I shouldn't be questioning it, I didn't want to be questioning it. But... did I even want to be friends with Annabelle anymore?

That's the downside of being best friends with your cousin. I'd never really needed any friends but Annabelle in my life... because, well, I knew she'd stay. She'd stay until the end of forever. I knew she'd stay – but then why did it feel so much like an ending when Annabelle invited herself over to brownie and hot chocolate with marshmallows Sunday night? It was like a time bomb ticking, ticking, the inevitable explosion nearing, second by second. The explosion that would rip up the grounds my life had been build on; the explosion that would shake my ground was nearing, second by second. Tick tock.

What I didn't realize was that all that was nearing was the blinding dark. An explosion lights up the world for the shortest moments, and leaves it, the ground shaken, used, left in the dark, the terrifying dark. Tick tock.

And then, Monday morning I was awoken by the constant ringing of my clock, as it ticked toward the moment where I would be standing alone, in front of an entire room filled with people silently judging me. Tick tock.

Monday morning hit me in the face like a solid brick wall – even though it really shouldn't. I shouldn't feel completely like a rabbit caught in the spotlight of a car, doomed. I shouldn't be afraid, after preparing for this day for days and days. I shouldn't be scared shitless, except, I was. I put on my cute shirt with the kitten eating a piece of sugar and brushed my brown hair in front of the mirror with shaky, sweaty hands.

Speaking of sugar I decided at breakfast that I deserved two spoonfuls of the sweet treat on my cereal today. I also shoveled the food down faster than I'd usually do – which, considering my horrible eating habits was way too quick, before I with shaking hands zipped up my jacket and found my sneakers, (Converse, of course, even though they weren't as fashionable now as they had been a few years ago) and slammed the door after me as I trotted down the stairs, down the streets, and to the place that was supposed to educate me with my skateboard under my feet as I glided over the street.

I stepped off my skateboard. Hearst High, it said on the sign outside of the school. A bird had shat itself on the "s" – 'Heart High'. I tried to smile – but the factor of cuteness about the sign was lowered drastically over the fact that the whole area was nothing but squares: grey, square buildings, square windows with grey curtains, grey, square bricks on the ground and only a few trees and small spots where the grass had been allowed to grow;

not exactly the place for romance. It seemed scarily dead outside on the grounds.

Mom would probably take that as a sign of students busying themselves with studies – but to me it seemed more like they were conspiring against the world. When you're in High School, you're either in, or you're out. It's a royal fight for the crown, with the same masquerade going on, year after year.

Right now they were building up the walls around the castle for the unlucky newcomers to climb and fight their way through the corridors as they tried to pursue the glory of popularity, risking their lives as they jumped from side to side, trying to avoid the fire from the evil dragon. With my luck there probably were serial killers walking around in there.

Okay, maybe that was a bit over exaggerated, but the grey walls really did invite that thought. I found the entrance, and slipped myself inside. I don't know what I had expected – perhaps that the corridors would be just as empty as the grounds outside. The air was thick with tension as girls gossiped in their tiny groups, - 'did you hear what she said about me', and 'yeah, totally messed up' seemed to be everything that was important to them - a group of boys were playing a random game with a basket-ball, perhaps practicing for sports after school, all wearing sporty clothes.

It was as if I was in a zoo – everyone was caged in their labels. The popular girls gossiping, the jocks playing sports, the nerds busying themselves with homework, leaning against a wall as they read aloud from a book – I wondered if they ever got tired of it, if they ever wanted to break free from the labels, be more than just the popular kid, more than just the jock, and not always just the smart guy in class. I almost felt bad for them, but I didn't have time to let myself get emotional.

I found my way towards the office following the small signs on the walls, until I reached the door. I was already awaited – a lady as thin as a stick was standing in the open door, her eyes sharp and cold, and her eyebrows bushy and furrowed tightly, as I presented myself. She extended a boney hand for me to shake. Her skin was white and slightly wrinkled. She steamed of danger – stepping one toe out of line would have long lasting consequences, I could feel that in my entire body.

"I'm Mrs. LaCreevy," she said calmly. "Your new English teacher."

LaCreepy? Must be mom's friend. "That's an interesting name, Mrs."

She did not reply. Perhaps she was used to people trying to compliment her in order to get a better grade – instead she started to lead me throughout the corridors, before she, just as the bell rang, opened the door to a classroom that for a minute or two buzzed with talking and throwing things at each other's head, just like they do in every classroom every single Monday morning. It wasn't before LaCreevy loudly said 'good morning' they fell silent. I had a feeling these kids only shut up in her presence.

"Do you want to tell the class who you are?" she asked me sternly, after she had made sure everyone was looking at me; she was cutting me out in pieces for the crocodiles to eat, she was trying to strip me down to the core, for them to look at me and poke fun. She was expecting me to know who I was.

"This is Emma, Emma Oaksby." She disappointed exclaimed when I didn't open my mouth. My lips seemed glued together, stapled together by an unknown force. Perhaps that was good – that way they couldn't judge me for anything except for the meat on my bones; all they could judge me on was how I looked.

Maybe if I didn't make a sound, maybe if I didn't move at all, the crocodiles wouldn't notice me. Although – I couldn't help but want them to notice me, just for the thrill of it. Just for the amazing feeling it'd be, when the adrenaline rushed through my blood when I tried to escape from them.

This is what they saw, even if I tried to go by without being seen; a girl with average height, average length of hair, – down to the shoulders - boring brown hair, baggy jeans, a skateboard under her arms, and of course... the oversize shirt with a kitten eating. The shirt that yesterday had seemed cute and comfortable suddenly felt very immature and stupid.

Mrs. LaCreepy – oops; LaCreevy, - pointed to a seat in the front, one of the most unpopular seats, and told me to sit down. I did.

Someone poked me in the back. I knew who it was, without even turning around – of course it was Her - the girl from the harbor. She was sitting there, her hair curled and brown, her eyes surrounded by a smoky makeup. Even though I somehow had known, it still came across as a chock – what was she doing here¬?

"Here," she said, and handed me my sweater. "Thanks for letting me borrow it."

I considered pulling the sweater over my head instead of the embarrassing shirt, but instead I pulled it close, hugged it as I buried my face in the fabric. It smelled clean, she'd probably washed it. "Adams, let Ms Oaksby look in your book."

The girl beside me moved her chair closer to mine, and pushed the book in between us.

I could feel Amy's eyes in my neck, almost burning me. How can you know who you are?

In the moment the bell rang and announced the end of the lesson, I jumped to my feet, rudely ignoring the girl beside me, to run for the door – the mysterious girl were leaving the room, packing her bag as she walked. I grabbed her arm.

"You've got a piece of me," I said with a pant, and sharply inhaled air through my nostrils; I felt surprisingly exhausted. Maybe it was something about her, making me tired. "Don't pretend that you don't. You took something, and you didn't give it back,"

She was smiling, a little, almost invisible smile, only just showing off her teeth, but yet a smile. I wanted to point out how she really could use a pair of braces – I felt shaky.

"I haven't got anything of yours." She said innocently, as she twisted her arm lightly, and took off. Tick tock.

"And you should get braces, you – you bunny!" I shouted after her. She didn't turn around. Maybe she didn't hear me.

Tick tock. Explosion nearing.

CHAPTER FOUR

No matter how much I sought, I could not find Amy anywhere on the school in that break. Or the next break, for that matter.

I spent that break searching for my biology classroom – in which, the girl from the harbor of course wasn't present in, even though I double checked the entire class to find her. I didn't really know if I had expected to be some kind of super-loner just like in all of the books about the pretty, perfect misunderstood girl with absolutely no flaws at all... if I had, I would've been disappointed greatly. I seemed to automatically receive the ticket as a 'temporary popular' girl: student after student were estimating my worth. I was temporary a girl that everyone looked at. I was exciting new in a dark world, a beacon of light in the dark world of gossiping High School students. I was fresh meat. If I didn't watch my steps, all that would be left would be my skeleton – they would rip me to the core, strip me for my secrets and poorly hidden opinions. Student after student in my year greeted me. Tick tock.

A pretty girl sitting beside me as I listened to – or, tried listening to, a teacher with the driest voice I'd ever heard, droning on and on about the photosynthesis which we'd probably all learnt years ago - volunteered as my guide around the school for the first few days. Tick Tock, explosion. She was a natural redhead - this did of course gave me reason to bring out the typical jokes about gingers – her hair braided in two, and with cute freckles all across the face, resembling the main character in "Anne of Green Gables". I instantly liked her solely for that fact – Anne of Green Gables was an adventurous, honest, curious girl, who would be faithful even if it would be the end of her.

The Anne-doppelganger asked me if I wanted her to reserve a seat at her lunch table with her and her friends for me – and as minute after minute ticked by, and she, in each break guided me around the school to make sure I attended my classes on time, carrying her heavy green bag around for my sake; after all that time passing on and on, I felt more and more stupid for not even remembering her name. She was brilliant though, very warm and inviting. I knew her last name was Stewarts – that was what the teachers called her. Tick tock.

At lunch she was waiting for me outside biology, just like she had promised. I felt a bit overwhelmed. Mom and dad had perhaps been right about this transfer… Maybe things would go right on this school.

So I ignored the tick-tock, and followed directly in her trail to the canteen.

Her friends called her Rock which I supposed was because of the way she seemed to be steady as a rock, holding her pack of friends together like a stapler keeping papers together. I could already feel the label sticking itself onto my face – less and less people started talking to me, as they already knew it; finders' keeper. Rock (whatever her name really was) Stewarts had found me. I didn't know where she was in the hierarchy of Hearst High – and frankly, I didn't really care. It felt nice to sit with her and listen to their talk about the boring teachers – apparently my biology teacher wasn't the only boring educator in this school - and the hot French substitute teaching math in third period was definitely also a subject they had to discuss. Two girls had a heated discussion – a brunette with amazing chocolate colored eyes was positive that his butt was the greatest she'd seen in forever, and the other girl (with a mop of curls making her look like a Disney princess) insisted that his French accent was just about the most amazing thing ever.

At one point the girl with the curly hair and brown eyes– Sophia – pointed out how they didn't learn anything in the lessons either way; the substitute seemed to have a IQ that seemed to be adjusted after his good look and cute accent ("Come on, you can't say that that French accent isn't glorious! It sounds so fucking attractive; I don't even know how he can have such a hot voice."

She said, as she stuffed her face with sandwich) - Apparently he wasn't all that smart. Lee Adams presented himself for me, before he made a joke about how the girls wanted Mr. Babin to speak French between their legs.

We all laughed, the two girls whining in disgust and making funny faces to make the rest of us laugh even more.

Usually I didn't like my own laughter; it always was too loud and obnoxious, but somehow, as it blended in with their laughter as well, I really liked it. It sounded like the kind of laughter that comes along with a hurting stomach and a blue sky above your head as you lie on the ground with your best friend. That was the kind of beautiful laughter this was. This was what I had been missing with Annabelle, sitting in a group, just listening to the others, without any expectations. I can't remember what we specifically talked about, even when I tried to think back to it, later that day during a math lesson from which I was excused for not paying attention since it was my first day. I placed my head on the table and tried to rewind that conversation at lunch with Lee Adams, 'Rock' Stewarts, Sophia and Cathy; when I tried to think of what exactly we'd been saying, I couldn't really remember anything but that joke about 'speaking French between your thighs' and that light, easy laughter, where my own giggles fit in perfectly, like a beautiful symphony. And I had been composing that symphony with them.

When school was over, Rock was waiting for me by the door to my class; she'd taking out the hair-bands around the two braids, her orange hair forming light waves down her back, and her bag over her shoulder. I felt completely exhausted – there were too many names swimming around in my head, too many students that had shook my hand and greeted me. It was all a little too much.

She offered to show me the easiest way back to the street since I was new, and I once again followed her through the corridors, my skateboard under my arm.

"So, what're you doing today..?" I asked, of course in the vain hope she'd offer me to hang out with her, of course in the hope that she'd smile and link her arms with mine and tell me that she didn't have any plans, and that of course she'd love to go to my house and show my parents that I had managed it through my first day on a new High School. Of course I was hoping that. But she didn't do that.

"I'm hanging out with one of my friends today," she said, "We're going to watch a movie, you know, me and her, and 'Sleepless in Seattle'." I just nodded, like a lifeless doll.

"Sounds awesome." She nodded back at me – we continued walking in awkward silence, as I considered slamming the board to the floor and drive away, fly away, grow a pair of beautiful wings and fly into the blinding sun. Fly away, like a butterfly, like a bird, like a desperate girl on her skateboard.

She pushed a heavy door up, and told me that we almost were outside. She said that in the very moment I realized that even though I had spent each break with her, I didn't know anything about her – or her friends for that matter. All I knew was that we all were fifteen years old and in our freshman year.

And then I saw her.

Ripped jeans and colorful sneakers, a long coat reaching her thighs, the long blonde hair tied in a bun, a couple of locks falling loosely around her skinny face, like a golden frame, the sun highlighting her hair. She was looking up at the sky, leaning her head back, her eyes squinting lightly. I looked up as well – a flock of birds were flying above our heads.

Louisa. My throat felt really dry all of a sudden, as I looked back at her. I hadn't expected to see her this early in the beginning of my new life on a new school.

"Hi Rock," she said. She looked at the ground again. I tried to break off a little laughter, and dusted off a bit of invisible dirt of my jeans. "Hi Louisa," I said, instead of Rock. She was looking curiously at Louisa, her eyes saying something I couldn't decipher, and raised her hand to pretend to put on a monocle. "It seems that know each other you do," she said, obviously referring to a movie. Louisa flinched lightly, and then smiled lightly, teeth just showing along with a cute dimple in the side of her cheek. Where had I seen that before..? She spoke up again, her voice a little shaky.

"Yeah, we went to the same school, before she transferred to another school… Which apparently was this one..?"

"Um, well it's awesome to see you again Louisa." I said,

"This is getting a wee bit awkward, so, um," No, no. Did I just say that? Stop blabbering. "Not like, I don't think you're awkward, just the situation is, you know, awkward." Louisa nodded in agreement, and bit her lip before she once again smiled nervously.

"We should go." Rock said with a calm voice, and linked her arms with Louisa. She – Louisa – waved at me just before they turned left at the first block and disappeared from my sight.

Louisa waved at me.

And then I heard it. A voice.

'Now, don't deny it.'

Amy? Was that her? But there was no one there.

Finally I could lay my skateboard down, and drive through the streets. Finally. Finally I was on the edge of something; finally I could feel like I was living. Although I drove slowly, it was a whole new world unfurling in front of me when I skated. A world that I was part of, but yet wasn't. An invisible world; a world that existed in my in-breaths and out-breaths as I drove there, on my skateboard, the skateboard that was there throughout everything.

CHAPTER FIVE

When I arrived at home I proved how my generation was totally and utterly fucked up – first thing I did, was to get online on my old Windows computer that most likely belonged in another decade. Not surprisingly I had received a bunch of friend requests on Facebook - from students I assumed now went to school with me, though I did not even know who most of them were. I couldn't recognize most of them by their profile picture either; I only accepted the people I knew I had seen; just like Rochelle Stewarts (Rock).

At least I now knew what Rock's real name was. I accepted the one from her, found Sophia that I had ate lunch with, and recognized a photo of Lee – he had called himself SeriousLee Adams, which was one of the worst attempts at a pun I'd seen in a long time; it was so bad, that it almost was funny. I smiled at the screen, before I continued scrolling. It was like I had become instantly popular. I had to remind myself of the fact that it only was because I'm new that things are like this right now multiple times. It was a little exciting and scary at the same.

I definitely was fresh meat for these students, I stated thoughtfully, as I scrolled down the list of friend requests. I could have spent the rest of the day wrapping the new books up in the brand-new bind that Mom had bought me, but I ended up checking out different profiles of my new class-mates that I apparently were to befriend – not only on the internet, but also in real life. A pretty girl with hair to her waist, kind of a real-life Rapunzel – she'd probably gotten extensions in her bangs or something; those beautiful locks couldn't be natural. I encountered a girl caked with a scary amount of makeup and a shirt showing off her impressive cleavage as well, along with a boy standing shirtless, showing off his abs.

Funny thing about social media is that everyone seems nicer and prettier than how they in reality are. I wondered whether I'd be able to recognize some of these girls next time I saw them; those profile pictures had probably gone through major photoshopping. Seeing things like that made me wonder if it, one day, would be possible to edit the real world; make the colors clearer, sharper, like a knife cutting a wound, making the blood shine, sparkle lightly in the edited sun that never would give you a sunburn, but only tan you beautifully. The world would be beautiful and clear, only made for the humans of this globe. Everything else would only be servants, only there to help the superior Homo sapiens.

The future didn't seem too bright for anyone. Was this really our sole meaning of life – destroying every single ray of sunlight, destroying the beauty in trees blooming and flowers on the beach; was this really our reason for living – covering the weeds that grow through asphalt, trying to destroy the life that made it through times of trial and hardship? Was this it? Was this all?

Something caught my eye – the chat line of people that was online; I rarely ever talked to anyone I actually knew in real life on these social medias – I was like a ghost, almost there, but not fully. I was fine with that – it was my parents that had a problem with it. Sometimes it was nice to sit there, looking at somebody's name and imagine who they could be talking to in that moment. Sometimes I wondered if their life really was as fantastic as they made it out to be. Sometimes I wondered who they were, deep down. That was the reason I was on this website, really. I was just as bad as them; I was there for the gossip too. I was there to keep my imagination going. I was there just for the sake of being there. People could say they didn't care – I could say I didn't care – but in the end of the day, we all cared a little too much.

But that wasn't why I couldn't shake my eyes of the little list of people. Louisa Coleman. She was – according to the green dot beside her name – online. My stomach did a lurch, as I reached for the computer-mouse and clicked on her name. The little pop-up box for the chat popped up, and I typed the three letters in quickly - 'Hey', my hand the next moment hovering above Enter, waiting for something I did not quite know what was. Perhaps I was hoping she'd send me a message first. Perhaps I was trying to devour the moment, savoring it in my brain to pick up on the sad days, to remember that one time I had messaged her and received a response...

I never sent that greeting; I never got that memory - for in that very moment somebody knocked on my door.

"Yes?" I called, as I moved my hand slightly and with a few clicks I had deleted the message.

My mom opened the door and stuck her head into the room, the rest of her body still outside my room, not crossing the very fine line of where I'd tolerate her presence in my room; no longer than one step into the room was my golden rule. "We're having for sandwiches for dinner tonight," – now I noticed the toast in her other hand – the one that wasn't holding onto the door knob. She raised it for me to see. "Come on out and get a sandwich, tell me about your day,"

She was munching on a bite of the sandwich, and asked, exposing her teeth that had small bits of cheese between them; "You on Facebook?"

I just nodded, and mumbled something about talking with a friend from the new school. Her eyes lit up in excitement. "So you've already made friends!" It wasn't even a question; it was moreover like a squealing school girl stating that she'd just gotten a new boyfriend, as she stepped closer to me, her arms reaching out in a slur of limps. She wanted to embrace me, but she'd choke me if she got the chance, even if she didn't mean to.

"Mom, go away!" I said; I didn't mean to, but I snapped like a snake striking against an enemy. She just nodded; her smile one of those a little bit creepy satisfied smiles which only mothers can pull off. I was – I'm sure she assumed - becoming normal. Growing up and whatever.

"What do you want on your sandwich?" she asked, swinging her hips from side to side, her eyes glinting with a mix of joy and a dangerous glint of offense. I asked her for one with pepperoni slices – the sort that I liked so much - and she nodded distantly as she stepped back, no doubt returning to the kitchen where she'd deliver the 'happy news' to my Dad over the phone and complain about my 'raging hormones'. I could already imagine her complaining though she still stood there in the doorway. She stood there completely frozen in the moment for a second or too, before she once again turned her body to face me once again.

"Also, Annabelle was calling your phone earlier, you left it in your jacket," She stated – luckily for her not saying any more about me 'making friends' - before she walked away with her crocs flapping against the floor. Tick tock.

I sat down on the chair again – but it was like I was a punctuated balloon – I didn't dare to message Louisa, even though I had the chance once again. I felt fine just looking at her name, I convinced myself of that, watching the green dot.

I found my pajamas, even though it wasn't my bed time yet, and brushed my hair, even though I felt like it was pointless to do so; I'd have to do it again tomorrow. I sat down in front of the computer again, and scrolled down the list of remaining friend requests. Mom came in with a sandwich for me, allowing me to eat at my room instead of coming out to her. Perhaps she did it solely because I had had a long day, trying to get to know so many people for her sake, perhaps she felt guilty for that. Perhaps she didn't want me to snap at her again, perhaps she could feel how tense I was, and maybe that was what hung in the air between us. She wasn't stupid. She knew something was up.

I looked at the green dot again. She was online; she was so close to me, only a few clicks with the mouse away. I moved the cursor a little, to hover above her name.

No. Stop it. Don't even think about it.

Tick Tock.

I had a dream that night. A dream – a nightmare – of the dark, built in the dark, created from a great lump of nothing, stripping me to the core. I was lying there, in the dark; I was naked, in the dark. I tried to raise my arm, but nothing happened; my entire body was tied together, like a knot. I could feel the dark scratching the outlines of my skin, crawling under my heart. The darkness clenched itself around me, like a fist, my legs was tied up; although I could not feel my limps, I knew that was what happened... and it scared me. My heart rate slowed, slowed down, more and more, preparing me for the slow death that was to come, as I suffocated in the dark corners of... ...myself.

And time ticked on and on, marching on without mercy. And my life had changed forever, even if I didn't think it had.

CHAPTER SIX

I awoke in the middle of the night- crying; the tears pouring down my cheeks, like waterfalls. Although I was crying, I didn't quite register that I was awake at first; there was dark everywhere. It took me some time to realize that I wasn't tied up, that my body was only mine; that I once again was in control over it, that this dark wouldn't tie me up. I laid there for a while, just lying there, as my eyes got used to the dark in my room. The dark in here seemed so bright and light compared to the dark I had just experienced in my nightmare – if it truly only was a nightmare, I thought terrified to myself. Don't be stupid, of course it's just a nightmare, I repeated to myself, before I mumbled it out loud – "just a nightmare," and clenched my pillow tightly against my body. I had curled myself up in a fetal position, my legs curled up against my stomach, and my arms holding onto my legs and the pillow as if my life depended on it. I needed to calm down, I told myself, as I pressed my eyes into my knees, until small red lights started to explode in the back of my skull. I felt light-headed and dizzy when I opened my eyes again to stare directly into the dark of the pillow covering my face slightly. I felt grateful for the dark; otherwise I would've been blinded by the sharp light. I raised my head to breathe in. Once again I buried my head in my knees; once again I told my heartbeat to calm down.

I didn't know why, but the dream scared me; scared me more than anything ever could. It felt like a thunderstorm; I had the same feeling in my entire body. That uncomfortable tingling, completely irrational fear of whether a lightning bolt would strike the house. I was waiting for the dark to strike once again, tie me up once again, swallow me again, making me disappear. I was waiting there, in the dark, curled up in myself, like a fetus.

It wasn't the first time either.

It wasn't the first time I'd woken up in the middle of the night, with tears pouring down my face and the silent sobs racking through my body as I clutched the thing closest to me to my chest; a book, a pillow, anything. It wasn't the first time I'd gotten up in the middle of the night to wash my face and pretend that the tears never had been there, as I did later. This wasn't the first time I'd grasped onto the sink at the sight of my face that stared back at me from the mirror, pale as a bone. Like a ghost. I didn't belong here, in this world, where the darkness would kill me if it got the chance.

But it didn't matter... right?

I didn't get a lot of sleep the rest of that night; to tell the truth, I couldn't fall asleep. I tossed and I turned, waiting for the sleep to take me away, fly me to Neverland where the dark never could reach me, where I'd be young forever, even after the end of forever. I spent that night with my head buried between my legs.

My cheeks were dry by the next morning; I was relieved to find that I hadn't screamed nor dreamt other scary dreams. Although the memory of the salty tears I had cried still resided inside me, like a demon waiting to break free, I decided that I couldn't let it ruin my day. Although I wanted to skip school; my entire body felt too heavy with fear of the dark, I didn't fake an illness. Mom probably wouldn't have believed me either; it would've been quite the coincidence for me to get 'sick' on the second day in a new school. I didn't want her to worry anyway – it wasn't like I had been bullied or anything else had happened, after all. The only thing that didn't fit into the perfect picture of my life was the dark. The dark, which no one but me knew about. It was the one thing that scared me more than anything else.

Once again, I would be fresh meat in school; and the lions would tear me to shreds if I stepped one toe out of line. As I stepped onto the street, I felt grateful for the plain black shirt I was wearing; even though it was vain to think so. I had the feeling that I'd be an outsider on this school if I wore more shirts with childish prints on it. I instantly decided to sort through my clothing in the moment I arrived back home. I was fifteen years old; I couldn't wear stupid shirts with stupid kittens playing with a stupid cube of sugar; that was what I kept telling myself, as I walked through the light rain that resembled my shameful tears that night. I could feel my vision get a little blurry of the mere memory. Not tears that stemmed from fear; these were of anger. I tugged a little at the hood of my jacket, and continued walking.

Rock Stewarts was waiting impatiently for me by the entrance of the grey buildings, linking our arms together within seconds of my approach, clearly stating that I was hers, before she turned to the entrance, her red- why was it even called 'red' if it was merely orange, I wondered – hair almost hitting me in my face. It hurt quite a lot as it had been braided tightly. I wondered if she always had it in those two neat plaits. I didn't know why she had even waited for me, and not just gone inside; I had arrived at that point in time where almost all the students arrive in a stream fighting to get inside first, and save themselves from the rain that seemed to be worsening every moment; perhaps it would evolve into a thunderstorm, I thought hopefully, as I glanced up at the dark sky. There was something calming about that... Rock tugged at me, and that was when the reason hit me - I was hers. That was why she had waited for me – I was hers. I didn't really mind that. She was my savior.

She wasn't my friend though; I could feel that in the air. We weren't friends – but yet I was hers. I was her property. She had offered what she'd give to buy me, and I had said yes.

This thought brought a picture into my head; slavery from before it had been abolished in America... The slaves had been sold at a market – what I remembered was a drawing of them standing there, as their soon-to-be masters took a look at them, deciding if they were worth buying. Sometimes a woman could be bought for sheer pleasure, and nothing more, a simple sex-machine. These women were just meant to accept it when their master wanted them to do things, because he – or she- was their master, owned them. It made me want to shake off Rochelle's tight grasp onto my arm. I didn't. Who cared if she owned me a little? That was what High School was all about in my opinion – getting as many friends as possible, owning as many people as possible. Hurt them before they hurt you seemed to be the golden rule. Break the person you love before they break you. That was High School in a nutshell.

I debated with myself why it was like that, as she clenched my arm lightly in her loose grasp. I followed her trail through the entrance, her pushing people out of the way, like a rock rolling down a mountain, unstoppable.

"Can I see your schedule?" she asked me over her shoulder as she placed a hand on another student's arm, silently telling them to leave, and tugged at my arm once again.

And then, with a last push from her side we were through the crowd of dripping teenagers, some of them dragging mud with them inside. Everyone jumped over small poodles of water; the weather seemed to become worse by the minute. She dragged me to a half-empty corridor. I fumbled with the buttons on my bag for a moment just to kill time before I'd have to move on again; I felt heavy and exhausted in my entire body. My legs ached, my shoulders hurt, my stomach felt as if it had been ran over by a bus. As if I'd tightened every single muscle in my body in my sleep. At last, when I'd reached the point where I couldn't drag out time any more, I found my schedule from the dark corners of my bag, completely crumbled of course; I never really bothered to put it inside a book or something. In my old class I had been forced to type in the schedule in the calendar on my phone, the reason being, that sooner or later I would have lost the schedule somewhere. I started to flatten out the paper (while Rochelle was clicking impatiently with her tongue) and handed it to the ginger. She looked at the plan and smiled softly, showing me the way to the classroom.

*

Perhaps the dark wouldn't leave me alone; perhaps the nightmare had crept under my skin and into my heart, clenching it, tying me up, just like it had done last night.

Or perhaps I needed to sleep so desperately that I'd do anything for it. Fact of a matter was- I fell asleep. And the nightmare returned. One moment I was trying to keep my eyes open to scribble down the formula on the black-board, and the next moment I had fallen asleep, and I dreamt - it was one of those strange dreams where you know that you're dreaming, but you can't wake up; I dreamt that I was back in the dark, and a piercing voice was hissing in my ear. I never knew what the words was; all I knew was that it scared me more than anything else ever could,

That voice reminded me of something. It reminded me of when I was younger, back when my parents wasn't divorced yet, and my Daddy had acted out simplified scenes from the bible in front of me. Not because he was a believer, but because he wanted me to know the stories. That was all it was, stories. Things people had made up, because they needed something to put their faith in.

It was the snake in Paradise, the one that had convinced Eve to eat the forbidden fruit. That was the voice I had heard whispering into my ear with a hissing, sizzling voice. I had heard my dad's voice. And perhaps that scared me even more.

CHAPTER SEVEN

Days passed on, slowly and tormenting. Slowly I was fading from people's thoughts, and though I still was referred to as, 'the new girl' by my teachers, people relaxed remarkably in my presence. Relaxed, as in – they ignored me. They didn't need to try around me anymore – they didn't need to be kind and welcoming anymore. If I earlier had believed that they had acted normal around me, I had been very wrong. They hadn't greeted me, but they'd noticed me. They'd made sure to laugh a little louder in their small groups.

Perhaps I was just paranoid. Wouldn't be the first time either. Fact of a matter was, I was becoming one with the wallpaper once again. Invisible, unless I, myself, acted out to become visible.

Once you've been in the spotlight, you want to stay there forever. Maybe that was what my mom had planned for me, thinking that it'd get me friends; – I started trying to get attention. I stumbled over my feet in the hallway in the hope that someone would help me pick up my books. I was hoping for that High School romance you see in all the movies; I was waiting for somebody to come along and pick up the books for me, touch my hand in the process and watch me fall for them, as soft music played in my headphones.

I was waiting for that sunset over the ocean, setting the sky on fire. I was waiting for someone to come running towards me like the end of a beautiful movie. I was waiting for the sound of a horse neighing loudly as it galloped with me, into the fairytales I dreamt of. And I knew exactly who I wanted to touch my hand. I knew who I wanted to watch the sunset with. I knew exactly who I wanted to be riding their own horse, riding beside me, and I knew which laughter I wanted to listen to.

But I didn't want to know. I didn't. I couldn't.

I wanted to be noticed again. Although the spotlight made me feel sweaty and nervous, I wanted to be there again. I was pathetically trying to get attention, like a toddler. The days passed, and I didn't even notice how my life was changing, slowly but steadily, as I fought my way through the crowd.

It wasn't just about the attention thing; that wasn't anything new. In my own, honest opinion; I was an attention-seeker; always had been. That probably was the reason I hadn't got any other friends than Annabelle. I wasn't your typical 'loner girl', sitting in the back of the class, neatly writing down her notes, like all good girls were supposed to do. I didn't fit into that image; I was too loud and obnoxious, but at the same time I was too good at pushing people away. I was the girl that had skipped an entire lesson to figure out how to climb the rooftop on the school building, and had clambered around it screaming 'I'm on top of the world'. A teacher once told me to never do that again which of course resulted in me crawling up on the roof again in the next break. Perhaps that was why Annabelle and I were such good friends – because we had the same blood of a rebel running in our veins. If it even could be described as being rebels – we were just dumb-asses, really.

So school felt extremely difficult to get through the next days. I didn't get enough sleep, afraid as I was of the nightmare to return – I couldn't forget it – and my constant craving for even the slightest sliver of attention not being satisfied. Furthermore I continuously ran into Amy. I didn't know if I wanted to talk to her, or for her to dissolve into the air. She scared me, but in a thrilling way. In a way that made me go for a run when I saw her in the hallways, but feel disappointed when she didn't chase me, simply because I was so darn selfish. In a way that was incredibly selfish, I wanted to be something special. I wanted Amy to talk to me – but at the same time I didn't. I wanted to rebel, bend the rules and live life dangerously, just like when I was flying away on my skateboard. Constantly on the edge, that was what I wanted. It was excruciating, wondering what would happen if I talked to her again. I wanted to run away – but I didn't want to want to run away. The more I thought about her, the more interesting she seemed to become, and the less strange her questions seemed to be.

So perhaps I was more relieved than scared when she, a Friday two weeks later, blocked my way out of biology. Amy.

She stood right in front of me, forcing me to either push her aside, or step away from the door, allowing the rest of the class to leave the room.

Perhaps it was because of my lack of sleep; perhaps it was just because I wanted someone to notice me. I didn't know why, but I moved, although the sight of her worried me; I had convinced myself that she wasn't a sign of danger, but looking into her eyes now, I felt nothing but fear in my entire body. Tense, ready to run, run far away as I suddenly knew I had to. I couldn't stay here

"Trust me; it's in your interest to talk to me." She said, her voice determined as she held onto my arm. It reminded me of how Rock held onto me. Amy owned me, or at least that was the signal she was sending me.

"Trust me, no matter how interesting you are, I don't want to talk to you. I'm trying to get integrated in this fucking place. I'm not fucking interested!" I hissed, trying to keep my voice on the down-low, my voice sizzling like a snake.

"You may not be interested right now… but what if… I told you, that I can help you stop the nightmares?" she said, her arms crossed, and her eyebrows raised triumphantly in the air, a smirk plastered upon her face, her lips puckering slightly as she blinked innocently a couple times. How did she know that? I stepped back – at first I didn't even recognize that I had done so; it was the sudden distance between our faces that did that I was able to breathe more freely.

It wasn't like I was afraid. She was only a few inches taller than me, and her body slender, she wasn't threatening in any way. I was not afraid.

I was just... scared, beyond that even; I was horrified. But she was promising me that my nightmares could stop, and for that, I'd do anything. Anything.

"Close your eyes," she said. I closed my eyes, shut them tightly until the dots of white light disappeared, leaving me in a comfortable kind of dark.

"Hold your nose with your hands so you can't smell anything," she said softly.

"Is this about finding my sixth sense or some other mind-fullness shit? Can't you just... wave a magic wand?" I asked grumpily, opening my eyes again to face her once again.

"Close your eyes." She said; her voice softer than ever, completely ignoring my rude remark. Her voice was dangerously soft.

"I'll hold your ears. Then we'll see what you can hear."

I raised my hand to my nose, and closed my eyes once again. And then I waited. Waited as time ticked on and on, not hearing, not seeing, not feeling.

And then - I was back in the dark. The dark that swallowed up the whole world, bit by bit.

The whole world was dark now. Not dark as in when you close your eyes; not a soft dark as the late summer nights at the beach, listening to the birds tweeting, neither was it a black dark as in the late winter days where you couldn't see your own hand even if you tried, not even dark as in your worst nightmares throughout your life, running from the monsters that would swallow you up.

This was a true, full, scary kind of dark; a darkness that went beyond black; a dark that crept into your body and soul. This was the kind of dark that was inside the creepiest, scariest closet in your childhood; this was the kind of dark that made your eyes watery. Slam the door, something whispered. Me? I didn't know. The door to the soul, your soul. Something slammed inside of me; I would've have sworn I was body-less if it hadn't been for that; the door slammed, my heart closed itself.

An empty place - an empty world, the remains of a majestic kingdom, a world filled with stories that had been put to a sudden end. This was my mind – but was it my kingdom?

Who owned this kingdom? Who ruled it?

What are you to do, when your worst nightmare comes alive, and you don't know how to escape it? What do you do, when a voice that you know so well crawls upon your skin, and catches the words you want to say before you even know it?

You already know what you are... don't you, abomination? The voice said in a hiss, crawling through my veins, running along with the blood inside me, or outside me, I didn't know. Was I bleeding? I didn't know, I didn't know, and I shook my head frantically; I knew I did so, but I couldn't feel it. I shook my head because that was the only thing I could do, because everything inside me screamed no. Nonononono. I can't. I can't, no. No. NO! NO!

And then my eyes flew open as I screamed. Screamed my heart out. Screamed and screamed although a pair of hands covered my mouth, and I was surrounded by light, and I felt blinded, and no, no, no.

"You said you could stop it!" I screamed into her face, my spit flying from my mouth... but I didn't care; nothing mattered except the broken promised. "You promised it could stop, you promised!"

"Calm down, it's a process!" she shouted, as I ran away. She was hurting me, she was hurting me, making me bleed from the inside out...

...a process. A process, a process, a process.

She had promised, hadn't she?

CHAPTER EIGHT

I wanted to skip the next lesson – English with Mrs. 'LaCreepy',; - but a voice in the back of my mind convinced me not to do so; she was mom's friend and she would with no doubt tell her if I skipped. That little voice also talked me out of putting on my headphones and listen to my favorite band. I admit it; it was hard to keep myself away from my phone and allow myself to be swept away by the beautiful voices, but it kept me out of trouble and kept me away from the principle's where I without a doubt knew I would have ended if I had dared to do any of the things I wanted to do. Instead I kept my head down, and neatly wrote down my notes, just like the nerd that I wasn't. But right now I was. Right now I didn't want attention.

I had gotten enough attention for the day.

I kept my head down as I walked through the hallways of the school. I kept my head down as I worked with algebra in math. I kept my head down as I walked home from Hearst High; I kept my head down as I locked the door up to my home, and I kept my head down as I walked through the house, only saying just the amount of words I needed to my mum before I left to my room.

I needed to stay away from trouble – trouble would require me to be noticed. And although I wanted to be seen, I could not let that happen. I couldn't. And I wouldn't.

Amy had noticed me, she'd seen me, and she had scarred my soul. I could feel it in my entire body; it felt like a giant knife was hovering above y body, covering me in open slits, letting the blood flood ever so slowly. I was bleeding, and I was hurting. But it was on the inside, where no one ever would look, where no one ever would see it. I kept my head down, because that was all I could do. Because I needed to save myself. The world was waiting for me to break down.

Not to mention, she had stolen something of mine. She had stolen a piece of me.

But then, when I opened my computer later that night, I saw something that made my entire body jerk away from the lit screen. It was something that made me unable to keep my head down for the rest of that day, although I still was determined to stay away from trouble.

And what was this something?

A message. A simple, short message, that made my heart beat a little faster, made me press my nails against my palm for that surge of pain, for the pain to wake me up; but it didn't. I was awake, and yet I was in a nightmare.

"I know you're scared." There was no name at the end; just that simple sentence, and above, a line stating, 'anonymous asked you:' (even though it wasn't a question), but it was no use to pretend that I didn't know who it was from. I knew it all too well. I could feel my hands getting sweaty as my hands hovered above the keyboard.

As the seconds ticked by, I could feel a drop roll down my eyebrow, as I stared. The screen was alit and blinded my eyes like the sun – or more like the depths from hell were shining up at me, the flames tickling my feet, the lakes of fire dragging me down

I buckled up my legs, to sit on my knees on the chair. All of a sudden, it felt too dangerous to sit 'normally'. Tick tock.

I closed the tab, and opened a new one.

A little pop-up window showed up.

You have received a message from: Louisa.

Louisa.

Want to hang out sometime? It feels kind of strange without you her in school. I've always wanted to talk with you, don't know why I didn't. Louisa, x

Of course I do. What about – I stopped to think for a moment – next Friday?

*

Later that night, when we – mom and I - were sitting comfortably in front of the television with a smoothie made of frozen strawberries bought from the supermarket, I asked her. I asked her the question I'd been burning to ask her for weeks now, ever since a strange girl had arose from the water and reminded me that there was an entire world out there, reminded me that I didn't know who I was. I asked her, although it was a strange and ridiculous question. A stupid question.

"What does my name mean, mom?"

She stiffened, her entire body jerking to a halt as she – while I spoke - stretched out to reach the remote to change the channel; she stopped completely, her body stiffening, her eyes placed themselves on me. I found myself truly creeped out. Mom never looked at me like that – usually we didn't even talk together.

"Who - who asked you that?"

Her eyes were the size of the moon, as one of her hands rose in the air to be put to rest on my left cheek, as she worried stared into my eyes, the TV remote forgotten for now. I wondered if she was assuming I had taken drugs or something. I had read somewhere that your eyes got bloodshot when you were high.

"Just… somebody in school," I said truthfully. I didn't even get to think about lying; the question came so suddenly and weird. I didn't even get to ask myself why she thought it was somebody else's question; I didn't get to wonder at all. I just replied.

"I, I – It doesn't matter what your name means Emma. It doesn't matter." She whispered, as she dragged me closer and squished me close to her chest, clutched me tightly in a big hug. It felt strange. Strangely nice.

You didn't have to be Sherlock Holmes to figure that my mom was hiding something from me.

Chapter Nine

The days passed by, and I got more and more accustomed with the school; I couldn't help but be proud of myself when I found my way to biology - all by myself (I even arrived on time, which was even better)! I learnt to quit bringing the skateboard with me to school; it did not make me cooler, which sort of was the foundational idea of even bringing it. I learnt which people I was supposed to avoid – who, not surprisingly, were the gossiping girls I'd seen the first day. Rock was releasing her grasp on me; I was now clutching onto her using all my might. I didn't want to be left alone in this world of dark gossip. I kept my head down as I walked through the hallways, half hoping that my silence would make me just a tiny bit more interesting, just like in all the movies. I was dreaming of my happy ending. But my story had only just begun…

I couldn't help but look forward to Friday where I would meet up with her – Louisa. We'd decided to meet at her house – she had sent me the address over Facebook, and I was practically counting the hours until the Day. I felt a little bit like a giddy child waiting for Christmas Eve, staying up all night waiting for Santa to come with the presents in the darkest hours of the night…

And finally it was Friday, and we were released from the hellhole they call school. I found my way throughout the streets –I had found the route to her house on Google Maps, and had learnt it step by step, without actually going there. The house looked like the houses from Harry Potter; the ones the muggles lived in, Harry's uncle and aunt. It looked terribly normal. Her family didn't like attention, I figured.

I caught a glance of a head through the window in what I assumed was the kitchen.

The curtains dropped again. Perhaps she was as nervous as I was, I thought, as I stepped up the few steps on the stairs to the doorway. That thought was strangely comforting.

The door opened at once, I didn't need to knock twice. She'd been expecting me. Although I knew it was because we'd arranged it, I couldn't help but feel a little fluttery over the thought. She'd been expecting me.

She reached a hand out to shake mine – luckily my palm wasn't sweaty, which I silently thanked a higher power for. We stood there for a moment, as we locked our hands together in the all-too-familiar greeting that felt a little too formal. We'd been going to the same school for more than seven years after all; we weren't supposed to be awkward with each other. Perhaps that was why she (awkwardly) shook her head a few seconds after the thought hit me.

"Can I hug you instead? Oh, also, do come in," she asked, and tugged lightly at my arm, rushing to close the door to keep out the cold fall air. I imagined a whirlwind bringing in all the leaves of the trees into the house, so that we'd have to clean up. She'd be laughing and joking about our bad luck I thought, before I stepped inside, the thoughts running through my head like water in a waterfall.

She spread out her arms to greet me in a hug. I leaned in. She was warm and nice; she had a nice clean scent about her, her hair smelling of apples. I buried my head in her hair for the shortest of seconds, nothing that took more time than a blink of an eye. I inhaled it, the smell of shampoo and apples, and I wondered why we'd never done this before.

My lips puckered lightly as we parted; I kissed her on the cheek. A brief touch of lips against skin, but a kiss nonetheless.

"I've actually really looked forward to this," she said sweetly over her shoulder, smiling a nervous smile that showed off her front teeth, as she gave me a quick house tour; there we had the kitchen, super up-to-date, looking like something you'd find in a starship; white and sterile, like in a hospital. I wondered if they could even find the oven in all those white cupboards and drawers. She showed me through the living room – I could very vividly imagine her sitting on that couch, relaxing after a long day, watching SpongeBob SquarePants – and pointed at a couple doors explaining who lived in there. "That's my parent's room, where basically they fuck when they don't fight – and that's my big brother's room, he's seventeen, and such a pain in the ass." She exclaimed as we passed the two doors. "Not literally, I mean. He doesn't rape me. Just… figuratively," she explained softly, her eyes shining in the short silence. "That came out wrong, huh?" I asked her, as I brushed a persistent lock of hair out of my eyes.

"Yeah, it really did." She replied, and opened the door to what I assumed was her room. "He's a skater like you are, but he won't teach me how to do it. I can only use a skateboard on plain road; he can do tricks and stuff like that." She turned her back to me for a moment to find the switch beside the door to switch on the light, and turned to meet my eyes once again. Her room was small, but bright.

"I'm kind of nervous," she admitted with a nervous laughter as she stepped backwards through the door, keeping her eyes on me – I didn't know why I didn't say anything. It felt amazing to stand there, watching her laugh. Her laughter was light and loud at the same time, like a river in the summertime continuing on and on, beautiful and natural. Trickling its way into my ears, her laughter made me want to squirm a little while it also made me want to dance, let all the feelings pour out of me through my steps and the smile that I couldn't hold back, even if I wanted to. I felt like crying of happiness.

"Check this out," she said, interrupting my track of thoughts about how amazing it felt, standing there. I stepped forward to see how she lifted up in something that most of all looked like a pile of pink cotton.

"What's that?" I asked her with a loud laughter – perhaps too loud; I didn't really think in that moment.

"It's a scarf..." she mumbled, looking down at the floor again, seemingly ashamed of herself. She was wearing eyeliner, I noticed. Again I couldn't help but smile at her. I wasn't sure why.

"I've been working on it, since I was like... Nine years old or something." She continued with a mutter, and looked up at my face again.

"That's cute." I mumbled – it felt like it was important to keep our voices on the down-low - and reached out after the pink 'scarf'. She handed it over to me for me to run my hands over. It was soft, and although the color was hideous, it was kind of cute. Adorable, really. I imagined nine year old Louisa sitting on the couch in the living room knitting on her scarf that never really would be finished...

"Want me to teach you? How to knit, I mean?" she asked – and before I even got to answer, she pushed me down on the bed, and threw a ball of cotton at me.

We spent the next hour or so trying to make me able to avoid stabbing someone in the eye with the knitting needles, and instead actually work on the pink scarf. It took a great deal of effort, and Louisa was harmed greatly in the process (I scratched her arm, which made us laugh louder than I remembered having done in a long time) – but eventually I figured out how to do it.

It took me some time to feel it – but at some point I couldn't help but notice that she was looking at me. Not at the knitting needles, not at the embarrassingly bright neon-pink scarf we were working on; at me.

She was looking at me, her eyes sending me a strange, beautiful message that I couldn't decipher.

"What?" I asked.

"You're beautiful," she said tenderly as she – just like my mum had – put her hand to rest on my cheek. It made me wonder.

I could feel it in the air; I wasn't supposed to say no, and I wasn't supposed to give back a compliment. This was more than a girl craving to be told that she was pretty. This wasn't a game about getting as many compliments as possible.

Yet I whispered it back at her. "You're beautiful."

Why? Because it was true; because in that moment I could see the beauty in life that you always pass off as nothing; her eyes the color of the sky in the fall, grey and blue mashed together like clouds forming strange figures – and I inhaled her scent as we leaned closer and closer; she smelled like lemons; fresh. Like spearmint toothpaste. Her hand rested beautifully on my cheek.

I didn't know what I would've done if we had continued doing whatever we were doing – leaning in, leaning closer, waiting to feel our heartbeats beat as one; maybe we'd have hugged, or maybe we'd have kissed – I didn't know what I would've done, if my phone hadn't beeped loudly in just that moment. We stopped instantly, our heads jerking away from each other.

"It's my mum," I said, already knowing before looking at the device.

The text said; "Are you coming home for dinner? Love, Mom"

Mom had ruined the tender moment. It felt like there was no reason to stay any longer. I didn't want to spoil what had been an amazing time by trying to build up the magic once again.

Yeah. I typed back.

"I better go," I said. She nodded, a little bit disappointed it seemed; I would've been too, if it was me. We hadn't talked about how long I would have stayed, but I'd definitely expected to stay longer than these few hours. But now the air was filled with awkward tension, and I couldn't ignore the feeling in my gut that told me to leave before I did something dumb.

She followed me to the door again, this time not talking at all. There wasn't much to talk about either, really. I got on my jacket and picked my back-pack up from the floor where I had left it when I senselessly had hugged Louisa. We stumbled through an awkward goodbye, and I turned to leave, - but stopped, when she spoke up. "Wait." She said. "Wait."

"Wait," she said for the third time, stumbling over her words; "can we do this again?" she asked, stepping forwards toward me, ignoring the cold fall air that gave her visible goose-bumps on her forearms.

I smiled. I couldn't help it – it just materialized itself onto my face, as I stepped backwards down the stairs. "Of course." I said. It felt so natural when she pulled me in for a last hug.

It wasn't before I had passed through three streets on my way home, the thought hit me. And it hit me like a bus.

She'd done the same thing as my mom. Were they together on something? Were they planning something together?

My mood dropped instantly. I waited impatiently for the street light to turn green, wishing I had my skateboard to calm me down, and make me look cooler. I needed to be on the edge right now. But yet I was already falling.

Chapter Ten

I was back in Louisa's house; it seemed even more warm and cozy than I remembered it, as I walked through the hallway once again, following her closely as she walked by.

"And that is my brother's room," she said, brushing a lock of blonde hair out of her grey-blue eyes, and pointed to the door to her left, and turned her head to look at me over her shoulder. "He's a total pain in the ass. Always shouts at me when I enter his room."

It was like the door was pulling me in, dragging me down as I stared at the wooden door. Danger is always intriguing. You try the rollercoaster at the amusement park a million times although it's scary – just to feel that rush of adrenaline, just to feel the fear, just to scream loudly and feel alive. There's nothing that makes you feel alive like that fear. That feeling of fear and excitement is something you search for everywhere. Everywhere you go.

"You should go in there, Emma," she said gently, and took my hand. It was warm and slick; her nails scraped lightly against my palm, manicured to perfection.

"I don't think that's a good idea," I whispered, and shook her hand out of mine, although I didn't want to. Something else held control of me. Maybe what I had said wasn't even a whisper; maybe it was just a thought. Maybe I actually talked; I didn't know. She looked into my eyes, hers a grey-blue color; and it was like looking at the sun – it blinds you; makes strange, weird shapes appear in front of you.

"It'll piss him off, won't it?" she said, and shrugged lightly. "That'll make it so worth it. What's life without a few fuming dragons – and a few fuming teenage-boys, huh?"

She took my hand once again, and carried it through the air to the door knob, and placed it there, clenching my hand tightly as she stepped back.

I stared at my hand on the gilded doorknob. Gilded misery. I pressed it – it was heavy, as if it wanted to keep me away from the dangers of that room, keeping me away from daring to do anything besides falling on my skateboard. I pressed, pressed, and suddenly the door swung open on its hinges. Just like that. It was empty; completely empty, the walls bare and white, the floor naked. There was nothing in this room. Absolutely nothing. It was empty, a lonely room somehow. Completely empty. Absolutely empty. I couldn't help but laugh at myself; was this what I'd been so afraid of? An empty room without as much as a bed, or a closet, or – or anything?

I stepped forwards.

And the dark

Swallowed

Me. Like a monster, like your worst nightmare. The dark had come alive, and it was ready to destroy me, fully and completely. It came out of nowhere; like bugs underneath a stone that I had whipped away, and now I were to be attacked by the many, many thousands of bugs, eating me up, sitting on my eyeballs, and I couldn't scare them away, because it was just dark, swallowing me up...

I woke up, gasping, almost crying in my hot bedroom, the air almost liquefied. I was drowning in the air. I was like a fish on land. I felt sick and there was no doubt in my mind that I was pale as a bone in the face. I could feel the cold sweat on my forehead, and tried to dry it off with my hand.

And at my feet, sitting there like a deadweight dragging me down, drowning me in my worst nightmares – was she. Amy.

"How did you get in here?" I asked with a hiss, and tugged at the blanket, almost expecting her to fall down the bed, but she stayed still in her place. Steady like a rock, she sat there, looking at me with her huge eyes, mysterious and pale, like the moon.

"Does it matter?" she replied lazily to me, her big eyes blinking innocently as she shifted lightly. She looked as though she'd sat there for a long time.

And it dawned on me.

She was evil, she was the dark. And the next thing I knew, she had jumped to sit on my stomach instead of at my feet.

"You really frustrate me Emma. You really do. I'm just trying to make you realize what you already know, but you just push me away!" she hissed the words into my ear as she pressed herself against me, now placing her legs over my arms which she held in a firm grasp. I couldn't breathe.

"You're stupid, Emma. You already know, but you just won't show." She continued, her voice almost echoing in my head as she whispered the words into my ear.

My arm hurt as she pressed her knee deeper into my flesh, her hand gripping my shoulder, nails digging into my skin under the pajamas shirt.

"You are feeling something special." She sizzled like butter on a frying pan, hissing like a snake, hissing into my ear that I was feeling something special, and I felt like passing out, like she was drowning me, drowning me in that liquefied air that suddenly was all around me. She was shaking my upper body, like trying to wake me up; maybe she was trying to do that, and my eyes were rolling and I had lost control and she was shaking me, or maybe I was shaking myself, I didn't know, I didn't know anything, and nothing made sense..!

Maybe I blacked out; all I knew was that suddenly I awoke in the middle of the night once again, this time without cold sweat on my forehead and without the feeling of being sick.

Amy was gone.

I turned over, and slept.

CHAPTER ELEVEN

I was running late the following morning, not registering the ringing of the alarm clock standing on the table beside my bed. To be accurate; I had heard it, but had somehow managed to shut it off in my sleepy daze. Mom had had to wake me up and all I could get for breakfast was a banana I ate as I tried to put on my trousers and pull a purple sweater over my head. Mom made me a quick sandwich with peanut butter and handed it to me as I pulled on my converses. I ran out in the light morning rain, cursing myself as I took a bite of the sandwich, which probably had been meant for lunch. I didn't take my skateboard with me; I knew I'd regret it no sooner than in the first break where I wouldn't have the ability to practice driving on that ruddy thing. I'd probably end up in the library instead.

And so I did. I ended up in the miniature version of a library the school had. One of the girls from my class guided me up the stairs to the few shelves filled with books, and a plump couch; that library didn't hold half the books I wanted to read.

Although I was sleepy and drowsy the first couple of hours (- I was so tired) I had expanded my mind. I had come to a realization. I didn't want to put up with bullshit anymore. I didn't want to be a victim of whatever Amy was going through in her own personal life that caused her to attack me. I wasn't going to put up with her little mind games.

In the second break between Maths and English, Rock followed me to the library as well, guiding me around the few shelves, showing me her favorite books, and found a Harry Potter book for her to read herself.

"I just love Harry Potter," she explained with a chuckle, "and in English I need a book to read, so naturally I'm choosing thy Harry Potter book," she continued, trying to pull off the old fashioned words, not succeeding. I laughed with her as she slammed the book at her head, cackling with laughter over herself. I found that she was the type to laugh loudly at her own jokes.

That realization made me wonder whether others ever laughed with her. Her eyes were shining at me, sparkling happily; her exposed teeth shining in the light; did she always look this happy? It worried me, but I didn't know why. Being almost unnaturally happy wasn't a problem, was it?

She definitely was as steady as a rock, I thought as we started our English lesson, sitting beside each other, her in her long sleeves and cute skirt, and me with a baggy sweater and with the feeling that I could've slept for hours.

*

That night my mum decided to visit me in my room. I was surfing the web and listening to a song from my favorite show which would air the next episode in a few minutes time. I was very impatient, and couldn't wait much longer to know what would happen this time, and was sitting as if sitting on needles, getting to my feet every other moment. That was when she knocked on the door; I had just stood up and was moon-walking around the room. She tapped at the door twice and opened the door, standing in the doorway, looking pale and nervous, a pack of chocolate in her hands.

"Hey," I said. She opened her mouth – and closed it again. It struck me how frantic she looked, stressed, somehow. I wondered if she was going to tell me off for not doing the dishes properly or something… but where did the pack of chocolate fit into the picture?

She handed me the pack, and licked her lips once as they quivered slightly. Once again she opened her mouth, but this time the words did not fail her. "I bought your favorite brand," she said, obviously talking about the chocolate, which I now noticed really was my favorite brand; it was that German chocolate I always begged her to buy although it wasn't exactly cheap. It tasted heavenly; I doubted even the sweets shop from Harry Potter, Honeydukes, could've done a better job on it.

She handed it to me, and for a moment we just looked at each other in an uncomfortable silence. I had the feeling she was about to speak, but she just merely shrugged and told me to enjoy watching the new episode on Pretty Little Liars. She turned and left, leaving the door open of course. For a moment I wanted to yell at her, but then I caught a glimpse of the back of her head - more specifically; her hair.

She was getting older too I realized; my stomach gave a gigantic lurch. Mum was grey-haired already. She was getting older; day by day she was getting older. Old people turned grey; all grey, their hair, their wrinkled, paper-thin skin, their eyes, and faded away slowly.

I closed the door silently; for some reason I didn't want to shout at her now. We rarely got on well, and lately we'd been so close. I didn't want to ruin that. I opened the pack of chocolate, sat down in front of the computer once again, and split the chocolate into small pieces which I started to eat slowly; it was delicious. But I couldn't help thinking, couldn't stop wondering, worrying. Why had mum given me a pack of expensive chocolate she usually wouldn't buy, and for no reason either, it seemed? We had nothing to celebrate, and even if we did have something to celebrate, she wouldn't have let me eat it in my room; she would've dragged me out to the kitchen table and force me to drink a cup of tea with honey and share the pack with her.

There was something odd going on.

And then it hit me.

She had looked guilty.

Chapter Twelve

Saturday morning, a sunny, hot day so unlike any other days in September, I called Annabelle. It felt like we hadn't seen each other for years, when she picked up the phone after thirty-six seconds where I had my eyes clenched as well as my fist on the hand that wasn't holding the phone. Her voice was very cool when she finally picked up, icy, cold. This was quite a big change from her usual self, which was warm and cozy, like a cottage in the woods. She was my happy place. Or that was what she had used to be, anyway.

I suggested taking a trip to the beach. Although it was turning colder and fall wasn't that far, it was a hot day and we definitely wouldn't be the only ones out on the beach. Her voice softened a little. Perhaps she had guessed that I didn't really miss her as much as I should. Perhaps she knew that a new school meant that she and I were drifting apart. Perhaps she thought I wanted us to drift apart. Did I? I didn't know.

Mom packed a basket with a blanket, sandwiches and water bottles for us, and I changed into my bikini at home. I actually looked forward to see Annabelle. I had never gone so long without contact. I hoped something would be different when I saw her. Maybe I hoped that she would decline five minutes before I left, then it at least wouldn't be my fault that we had drifted apart. Then it would be because of her. But that was selfish and stupid.

She didn't decline though. At 12 o'clock she arrived with the bus, and we took another bus to the beach, complaining about the heat and trying not to giggle at the people in the bus which all seemed very funny for some reason.

We dived straight into the water; it was so cold that we yelped out loud, screaming and laughing as we spun around, getting dizzy and high on laughter.

She splashed the water directly in my face, showering me in droplets stemming from her hands. I clenched my eyes tightly shut, and splashed back at her, laughing. Laughter was my drug and I was addicted.

I didn't need to end what Annabelle and I had together. I didn't want to end this friendship. She was three years younger me; she was young and free, and I was burdened with darkness and hurt. I was scared, she was brave. We were opposites and yet we were so much alike, the same blood ran in our veins.

I held my breath and dived down into the water my hair flowing in the water above me. The world became fuzzy as I swam back and forth. I felt like a mermaid; swimming smoothly in the icy water that now felt warmer.

As we dried ourselves up with the towels I saw the back of a girl wearing a black and red bathing suit that was very tight on her after being in the water. Her shoulder-long brown hair reminded me of someone. "Amy!" I called. The girl didn't turn around. Either it wasn't Amy or she was ignoring me. I wanted to run up to her and wave my arms in front of her, force her to understand that no one messed with me. I wanted to tell her that I was tired of putting up with her and her dark powers over me, that I was tired of always drowning in myself. But I didn't.

I remembered my mum, how she was growing old. I wanted to help her, wanted to make her live until the end of forever.

"Do you think it's possible to stay young... forever?" I asked Annabelle, drawing shapes in the sand with my finger. A heart broken in two pieces and then a band-aid stitching it together.

"You've been reading Twilight or something right?"she said, rolling onto her stomach and looked me in the eye.

"The only way to stay young forever... is to die."

*

I spend that evening at home alone; practicing in the garden, trying to learn how to flip my skateboard in the air as I jumped. It was tricky to do this without, as my mom would undoubtedly call it, knocking myself up. I had fallen more times than I could count when my mum came out to me.

"I've baked a brownie, come in and have a slice and a cuppa tea," she said, as I jumped for umpteenth time. I shook my head, and she looked disgruntled.

"I know you're busy trying to learn to skate and knock yourself out, but I really need to talk to you," she said with an annoying voice of a know-it-all. Although I had just thought those words myself, I couldn't help but get annoyed. I wasn't trying to knock myself out. I was practicing. The fact that I probably at some point would've ended up knocking myself up was just a side effect. "No thanks, I really need to practice." I said, putting pressure on the last word, knowing that she'd notice it. She sighed deeply, and my stomach gave a lurch. There was something I didn't know, I knew there was. Something that made my mom look very worried, old and weary.

"There's something I have to tell you."

At these words I fell over the skateboard and scraped my knee on the stone floor, but I didn't take notice of it as I quickly stood up and said, "You have my attention,"

She looked at me, noticing how quick I was at agreeing and smiled wearily. Worn down.

She insisted that we made a cup of tea with honey for each of us before saying a word. We sat down at the living room table. I slouched myself in the comfortable black couch as I waited for the tea to be ready, anticipating her to speak. She did not say anything before the tea had cooled down and she had found a pack of chocolate cookies. Then finally she said, "Whole."

"A hole?" I asked disbelieving. This couldn't be what made mum look so tired.

"No, whole. That's what your name means." She said, sipping at her tea, holding at the cup with both of her hands, warming them. I nodded at her. Okay. My name meant 'whole'. Big deal. "That's not what I wanted to talk about," mum said, then corrected herself. "Yes, it kind of is about that."

I sighed deeply and drank from my cup. The tea was sweet from the honey. Almost too sweet, just like mum was too kind. Mum had staged this whole thing. The tea, the cookies, the chocolate she had given me... it was all staged, and it all came down to what she was about to say. I was about to know the truth.

"Everyone meets a... a person that changes their life-", she started, stuttering a little. "This is not about 'the birds and the bees' right?" I interrupted. She shot me a glare, and I fell silent.

"When I was around your age I met a boy, and he... yeah, well, he made me realize who I was. Everyone meets someone like that. I'm not sure what they are, I'm not even positive they're human... They're so angelic and so beautiful... Too beautiful." she looked dreamy; I could see her getting lost in thoughts.

"When you came home the other night and asked what your name means I knew you had met someone. That's a common question from them. As you know, my name is Abiageal, grandpa is Irish. That means joy; Aashiq helped me realize that that's what I'm supposed to be. I'm someone that is trying to bring joy to other people's life."

"Where did you meet him – Aas- whatever his name was, where did you two meet?"

"I was on a holiday in Africa with your grandpa and grandma – Aashiq is an African name." she didn't seem to want to go into detail. This wasn't a time for storytelling. We sat in silence.

"Do you like him?" she said and sipped lightly at her cup once again. Him?

I didn't say anything, I just nodded. We sat in comfortable silence once again before I said, "So, it's always a boy?" and linked my hands with her, like we were some kind of BFF's. "For the boys it's a girl of course, but no matter their sex, they always help you realize... who you are, I guess."

That night I couldn't fall asleep. I just lay there, staring up at the ceiling, wondering, worrying.

Amy was, according to mom, supposed to help me find the missing piece of my soul... but she was drowning me instead, killing me; not saving me.

CHAPTER THIRTEEN

Fingers were creeping over my skin, making my goose-bumps spread, the cold living in my very skin.

My legs were tied together; thick ropes of dark draped around me like a blanket, but so tight that I couldn't breathe, so tight that I couldn't think or feel, I couldn't feel a thing but the pain of the tight ropes that wasn't really ropes but just dark, killing me slowly. I could feel the tears rising in my eyes, warm and big. A tear slowly rolled down my cheek. Another followed. And another. And another. Fuck,

All the Dark wanted, was to be alone with me... forever. Just it and me, swallowing me up, together forever, in all eternity, to infinity and beyond. This dark was the dark of the lonely, of the ones screaming alone, of the baby left on a doorstep... This was the dark of the forgotten souls. And I could feel those souls' screams, creeping under my skin, tugging at my heart, dragging it down.

And then, just like that – I woke up, choking on the air that felt liquefied, drowning in it.

I didn't know why; maybe I could feel the presence of someone, or something; I looked to the window. A shadowy figure were sitting on the windowsill, jumping catlike out of the open window.

I jumped to my feet and ran silently to the open window, which was gaping widely, moving slowly because of the wind. I looked out of it - there was no one..? No shadowy silhouette running, not as much as a cat. There was complete silence except for the occasional car speeding through our street, although it was four in the morning.

I went to bed, drifting off almost immediately, falling into deep, deep sleep, dreamless and empty.

*

When I awoke the next morning the first thing I did was to look at the window. It was closed.

I dressed and debated with myself whether I should wear makeup or not and finally decided against it. My phone was lying on the windowsill. I didn't remember placing it there. I decided to send Annabelle a text to say thanks for yesterday. It had been amazing. It was one of those days you know you'll look back at when you're old and wrinkled, thinking that no matter the hardships, that moment, that day, that that time had been perfect.

"Thx for yesterday, had a lot of fun, we gotta do that more often," I typed quickly as I walked down the stairs and out into the kitchen where my mom was eating yoghurt from a bowl. I found the oats and prepared a breakfast for myself, oats with raisins and milk. Mom looked at me from the corner of her eye. She thought I couldn't see, but I could. I knew we both were thinking about what had happened yesterday. What she had told me. That thought sparked my curiosity once again, and I realized something. Amy was supposed to be a boy. Why wasn't she a boy?

Ten minutes later I was off on my skateboard in the chilly morning air. The sky was a deep blue; no clouds were to be seen in the horizon.

I spent the first break outside, enjoying what might be the last day of warm weather. I had borrowed a book from the library earlier that week and sat alone at a table, reading The Fault in Our Stars, which I couldn't help but love. It was a story about a girl with cancer, Hazel Grace and her romance with Augustus, a former cancer patient. Hazel was very sick, the story very sad and very beautiful.

In the end of the break I decided to take a stroll around the school, to learn my way around it.

As I walked around the building where P.E. took place, I heard something. Someone, to be exact. I heard a soft whimper, a sobbing sound... someone was crying. I followed the sound to the back of the building, where I stopped dead in my tracks. I had been right. A girl was sitting there, with hair as orange as carrots, braided into two fine plaits.

"Hey," I mumbled as I slid down beside the girl. I heard a light sniffle and the girl looked up with big teary, green eyes, once again resembling Anne from Green Gables.

It was Rock – and she was crying. Rock was crying. I didn't know why it came across as such a chock; perhaps I'd been expecting another freshman, crying over her first boyfriend that left her for one of the cheerleaders or something like that; I definitely had not expected Rock to be sitting there, up against the wall, looking at me with those big teary eyes, before she once again buried her head in her hands, shaking lightly, and a whimpering noise coming from her, falling, spinning out of control along with her light sniffles to keep the tears in. I could see dark spots on her knees, which I supposed was wet from tears.

Perhaps Rochelle "the Rock" wasn't as steady as I had thought she was. I sat down on the grass beside her and took a deep, sharp breath through the nose.

"What's wrong?" I asked gently, touching her shoulder in an attempt to calm her down. She shook it off. I felt a twinge in my chest, but tried to remember that she was upset and most likely didn't mean to hurt me. I couldn't get mad at her for rejecting my help. How was I even supposed to help her?

"Nothing," she said - her eyes still watery. I wanted to walk away in that moment – it felt too private. A tear rolled down her cheek. I reached out to catch it on my finger and awkwardly dried her cheek.

"Sometimes it's just difficult to fit in, you know?"

"You don't have to fit in," I replied – I didn't know what else I was supposed to say, even though I knew it was pointless to say something like that. It was a lie. Everyone had to fit in, everyone was trying to fit in, and if someone followed their dreams; stepped outside of the box they were fit into, they'd be disowned by the majority of people, avoided everywhere. Saying that someone didn't have to fit in, was bullshit. Fitting in was the only option there was.

I leaned sideways and caught her body which was falling onto me, caught her in a warm, passionate hug. I sat there, holding her quivering body. She was racking with sobs now. I was going to keep holding onto her, hold her as long as she needed me to.

She wasn't Rock anymore. She was Rochelle.

Chapter Fourteen

I held her for so long, clutching her to my chest, letting her cry bitter, salty tears on my shoulder. She was soft and warm, her body slowly relaxed as the sobs grew slower and less frequent. Slowly, silence fell as she occasionally hiccupped with tears overflowing in her eyes. When she had calmed down, (I noticed how silent everything was - we couldn't hear the other students anymore, perhaps lessons had started now?) - I took her hands in mine and said, "You're amazing Rochelle. You just can't see it yourself, which is why I'm here to tell you. You're amazing."

She just withdrew her hand and tugged down her sleeves. A thought struck me. What if she had-?

I reached for her arm and with a quick movement pulled the sleeve back. She had band-aids on; and there were scars. Not many, but a few pink, raw scars that looked maybe a couple weeks old. She had cut herself. She had cut that soft, beautiful skin of hers. She had actually put a blade to her skin and pressed it. I felt sick.

She flung herself unto me in that moment, her arms around my neck once again and buried her head in my shoulder.

"I just tried to take away the pain," she sobbed into my shoulder. Her feelings seemed too deep to cry now. Perhaps there were no tears left in her. She had cried enough.

"I know," I told her as gentle as I could, running my fingers over her hair and stroke her back slowly, calming her down once again. She sniffled and dried her nose. "I should probably get to Physical Education…" she said with a sad expression. She wasn't going anywhere I decided. I pulled her back into a hug.

She pulled back and said, "Seriously, I've got to get up and do something."

"Yeah, alright," I said, but continued, very firmly, "But you're not going to P.E. You're skipping today." She smiled, for the first time today, she smiled. She looked relieved. "What're we doing then?" she asked, clearly letting me take the lead.

"We're going to buy some chocolate and eat it with delight. Diets can wait till next week," I said, just as firmly. She opened her mouth and closed it again, but seemed to decide that it was better to let me have my way.

We left the school grounds and went to a shop just a few streets away and bought a pack of dark chocolate and a bottle of a soft drink. We walked to the park and ate chocolate, sitting on a green bench. We spent two blissful hours together, and I didn't think once about Amy, or angelic helpers, or anything really. I let myself loose, lived for each moment.

We spent the time that would translate to two lessons in that park. Although I wasn't in school I learnt so much. I learnt that when you drink and laugh at the same time the soft drink comes out of your nose and bubbles like crazy; I learnt that your cheeks can hurt from smiling; I learnt that there is nothing better than laughing with someone that truly want to hang out with you; I learnt that scars are battle wounds that deserve to be kissed… It was wonderful.

We returned to the school in the second break, between P.E. and English.

When I entered the classroom with Rochelle I pulled out my phone as I sat down and opened Facebook on it.

And when I opened the app I saw something. I had received a message. A message from Louisa. I could feel my eyes widen as I clicked on the message.

"Hey, I wondered if you want to hang out sometime this week…? Love, Louisa."

My hands shook lightly as I typed out, "Of course, would be awesome. What about Thursday?"

For a moment I started at the screen before I continued. "Looking forward to it. <3 x"

"Thursday is fine with me. See you then."
My stomach gave a lurch.

CHAPTER FIFTEEN

The days passed on too slow. I wished for time to pass on quicker, but for some reason the hours seemed to drag on and on as I sat in my chair in school, every minute seeming longer than the last. It seemed that dinner that night lasted forever. Although the food was delicious and mum was super sweet and asked me about my day, it felt like torture. The next morning, after a night spent in the company of the blinding dark that had tied me up once again, breakfast dragged on. School seemed unbearable even though Rochelle accompanied me in each break, telling me stupid knock-knock jokes and discussing the latest rumors about Jake Thompsons – apparently the king of the school as well as captain for the local soccer teams – and his breakup with Jessie-Bell Peters - the perfect queen bee with long blonde hair and deep blue eyes that charmed everyone she met. She was a ballet-dancer, Rochelle told me, as we walked around the school buildings thrice. She talked so much that I didn't need to do anything but hum lightly, and nod whenever she looked at me. I felt a little uneasy. What I had seen a few days earlier didn't fit with Rochelle being happy. I supposed she was acting happy.

"You don't have to act happy you know," I said softly, and placed a hand on her arm as we walked around the P.E. building where I had hugged her as she cried. "Not with me. It's okay to be sad around me." I stated just as gentle and moved my hand away once again.

We ended up sitting against the P.E. building, both crying. Maybe out of all the sorrows and thoughts that haunted us; perhaps because of happiness… we had each other. The sobs racked through Rochelle's body as she sniffled and coughed herself through the sorrow. I could see her drowning in her own sadness. My own vision was blurry and the tears fell steady as I hugged her, held her close and thought to myself that I'd never let go, I'd never let go of my fragile, beautiful friend. She was my friend. I loved the sound of that; friend was such a beautiful word. It fit perfectly on her. She was my friend!

She whispered something that I at first couldn't hear. I asked her to repeat it; she was mumbling into my shoulder as she hugged me for dear life.

"I think I love you," she whispered, repeating her earlier words. I jerked away. "No, no, no," I cursed under my breath. "This is not happening!" I ran a hand through my brown hair, the fringe kept irritating my eye. "Stop it, right now," I hissed to Rochelle and crawled backwards. She looked distraught into my eyes with her green ones. They were big and sad, filling with tears. It seemed that she couldn't stop crying.

"I love you too," I said awkwardly and scratched my chin worriedly. I didn't like to see people cry, especially not if it was my fault and especially not if I could do something about it. But what was I supposed to do? Lie to her and say that I liked her back? I didn't even like girls. How could she think that I wouldn't be at least slightly disgusted? I was so obviously not gay. Liar, a soft voice whispered. My dad's voice, the voice of the dark, and I was reminded that I had lost a piece of myself and I couldn't get it back...

"I love you too, I really do, but just not like that," I said with a quivering voice and moved sideways, away from her. She looked desperate, desperate and sad. Then, her expression changed completely, and she began to laugh, too loud. Just a tad louder than it usually would've been, and I knew – or at least thought – that it was a fake laugh.

"I don't like you like that either, stupid you. You're so funny; I don't like you like that. Not at all. Love you, but like a friend," she said, braiding her flaming orange hair into a plait thus avoiding my gaze.

I wasn't so sure I believed her. I was going to pretend I did though; it was the only way to stay friends with her. I was disgusted over her, but after all… I did love her. Just not in a relationship kind of way. I wasn't in love with her. But I loved her. She was lovable, how could I not love her, despite her scars and wounds. That reminded me of something. I rolled up her sleeves and saw satisfied that there were no new cuts. I was relieved. She hadn't cut that baby-soft skin. Apropos baby – "your skin is like a baby. You wouldn't cut a baby, would you?" I said, thinking of a song I once had heard; something about loving your body as your mother loved your baby feet. She was still crying lightly, sniffling every other moment to keep the tears in. I was surprised she hadn't already cried her tears out; I would have expected that her eyes would be dry by now. She just sobbed into my arms, while I thought that I loved her, that I would help her, even if it was the last thing I ever did. I was not letting her kill the child inside her. She still had the chance to get happiness. But… But…

But why would she think I was gay?

*

Thursday couldn't come quick enough. I knew that was what made me so squeamish about everything. I couldn't wait to meet Louisa again.

Finally it was Thursday, and I could run to the bus stop where the bus arrived just at time, jumping onto the bus just before it drove away. I was on my way. I breathed hard through my nose and exhaled. My side stung. I had been at a math lesson where I had had to deal with fucking algebra, which, in my opinion, was one of the worst things ever. I had been delayed as the teacher decided to give me extra homework. Apparently I would fail math if I didn't do this homework. I just didn't like numbers and formulas. I sucked at math, and mum would be furious if she heard that I was close to failing. I had to do this extra work.

But that didn't matter now. I was on my way to meet Louisa again.

And was the best thing in the world.

*

She opened the door the moment I knocked, almost as though she'd been waiting impatiently, looking out of the kitchen window, waiting for me. But then again, perhaps she was just bored, and wanted to hang out with somebody. It didn't necessarily mean she wanted to hang out with me. I could feel my good spirits drop a little, before I reminded myself that she had asked me to hang out with me, which was a pretty safe indicator that she liked me.

"Hey!" I said, and raised a hand to give her a high-five at the same time as she leaned in for a hug. The result was that I ended up hitting her temple, and she swayed back and forth for a few seconds before she staggered backwards. I apologized numerous times as I entered the house and took off my shoes and my jacket. Once again I was standing in her house. It smelled nice, just like a home should, I noticed. I hadn't noticed the last time I was here, perhaps because I had been so wrapped up in Louisa. She led me the way to her room once again, and we sat down on her soft bed, covered in white bedding. I felt too nervous to stay there though, so I quickly got up and wandered around the room. I couldn't remember much of it from the last visit, Louisa's eyes had been way too beautiful to look away from, a sight that no view could compare to.

Not that there was a lot to notice. The walls were plain and white except for a few posters of what seemed to be her favorite bands, a white desk in front of the window and a couple white shelves on the wall opposite the bed and a closet beside the door.

"You're crazy beautiful," she said, as she sat there on the bed, looking at me with a soft, gentle smile on her lips, showing off the little dimple on her left cheek. She was the one who was beautiful, I thought, but I could feel a smile spreading across my face nonetheless, and I had to turn around to hide it. I didn't want her to think that that had made me happy, for some reason I didn't want her to think that she had power over me. I let my hands run over the shelf in front of me.

"I'm about as significant as wallpaper," I said with a laugh and fumbled with the fine bottle of perfume I now picked up. It was shaped like a flower with purple and pink petals. The package beside it claimed that it was Someday, by Justin Bieber. My lips twisted into a smile. I didn't really know why that smile planted itself onto my face. It just... did.

I smelled it. It smelled flowery and of warm summer-days. I liked it. I turned around and asked, "Can I try it?"

She just nodded, and I sprayed a little perfume on my wrists. "It smells nice," I said. "I like it." She nodded, and made a gesture that obviously meant I should sit down beside her. I sat down beside her, inhaling the smell of flowery perfume, the very same perfume I had just prickled onto my wrist. Our hands were lying very close to each other, only a few centimeters. It was just a few centimeters between us.

Our faces were a bit too close to each other; it was like my breath got tangled with hers second by second, minty and fresh. She smelled nice, of shampoo, mint and something else, perhaps bare skin. My fingers moved slowly, crept shakily towards her hand. Slowly, slowly they moved toward her hand, so slowly that no one else would take notice of it, but just fast enough that I dared to do it. Only a few inches left before my pinkie would be touching her thumb; my whole world revolved around those few inches. I touched the finger with a burning feeling myself.

It lifted a little. My heart skipped a beat; my breath got caught in my throat for the shortest of seconds – nothing I ever would miss, that lost second. My hand climbed beneath hers before she could get to change her mind, the slender fingers locking around mine, tangling like our in-breath and out-breath, and our eyes - our eyes got closer and closer to each other, her gray and blue eyes, which I never really could specify as one color, so beautiful. Her lips were so close to mine I could almost taste them. She probably used lip balm – a lip balm with lemon; she smelled nice, fresh. Clean, beautiful, as her eyes started to close, the lashes fluttering on her skin like the fragile wings of butterflies in the summer.

I swallowed the piece of gum, swallowed my spit, swallowed my pride as I leaned in, and she was leaning in too. Unconsciously, perhaps, but we were nearing each other, gravity was pulling us closer, closer, and I didn't care why she was doing it. And there they were, her lips, tasting of faint lip balm and spearmint, her skin so close to mine that I could feel the tension, the friction.

We were bathing in each other, her warmth showering me like water as we pulled each other closer.

And in that moment, I swear I knew who I was, in that moment I didn't miss any part of me; on the contrary I knew I was fulfilled. I knew. I understood. I understood that wallpaper is very significant.

Chapter Sixteen

Her lips were soft against mine, so soft and tasting of lip balm and spearmint gum. Her hands were soft from what undoubtedly was a quite big arsenal of creams. Her nails were short and down-bitten; she had a bad habit of biting them, and the wonderful idea that she had bitten them in nervousness over meeting me floated into my dazed head. I had pulled her closer, and we were now sitting closer than ever. I wanted to scoop her up and cradle her tightly in my arms, her seated on my lap, but I also didn't want to break away from the sweet, innocent kiss. This was my first kiss, and it was everything I had ever imagined it to be.

Except that it was with a girl.

I finally mastered up the strength to pull away – not that there was much to pull away from. Our lips had been connecting in nothing more than a light peck, that had lasted so much longer than the pecks you give your old mom because she's bought you a pack of delicious chocolate (I hadn't even kissed my mom as thanks for the chocolate, I realized with a sting in the heart) – a peck that lasted forever, but yet was too short. I loved the taste of her, but I also hated it. I pulled away, and placed her hand in her lap as I watched the way she slowly came back to Earth. I wasn't the only one who had been completely blown away at the taste of her lips. For a second I smiled to myself, before I reminded myself that these feelings were wrong, so very wrong.

She opened her eyes slowly, her lips still puckered slightly. Her eyes were gleaming, and her eyelashes were fluttering lightly on her skin, like small black butterflies. She looked beautiful, like a sunset setting fire to the ocean. She was amazing, I realized, with a lurch of my stomach. It felt like my whole body was twisting and turning. A very unpleasant sensation.

I lifted my hand from hers, awkwardly scratching my forehead with it, and said, "I better get going. It's getting, uh, it's getting dark." The sky outside the house was as blue as ever, and there were definitely still an hour or more, before it would be twilight. But Louisa did not point that out for me but just nodded and ran a hand through her dirty blonde hair. I wanted to run my fingers through it too, it looked so soft and pretty, hanging there, reaching her shoulders. There was no sign of the little dimple in her cheek. That felt like a bad sign. I got to my feet, and looked at her with a look that clearly asked her to lead me the way back out. She slowly got up. Her eyes looked dead. There was no sparkle in them. She led me the way back to the hallway where I slid my feet into my shoes and got on my jacket before I walked out in the cold fall air, quickly considering to just walk off and wave goodbye instead of hugging her, but my decency got the worst of me, and I turned around.

We hugged briefly, our bodies barely touching. I wasn't sure I would be able to leave if I let myself get involved in that hug. I wanted to stay, but I also really did not want to stay. I loved her (loved?) but I also hated her. Hated her, for all the emotions she made me feel, hated her with a burning passion.

I couldn't be sure, but I thought I heard a sob as the door closed; a sob of desperation and sadness, a sob that definitely would be followed by a waterfall of tears. But it was probably just my imagination, wishful thinking that she wanted me to stay.

I walked around the city with my hands in my jacket. I somehow did now want to go home. Mom wouldn't be expecting me home this early anyway. I walked here and there, not really registering where I was. No matter where I ended up, I'd be able to find my way back; I knew this small town like the back of my hand. Lately I had very been frustrated about how small this town was. Gossip spread quickly throughout it. People knew each other; everybody was recognized when they walked down the street. I had never really thought much about it, but when I, in this moment walked down the streets and an old lady shouted,

"Hello Emma," from her garden, I really, really hated this city. I just wanted to be alone in peace, just walk around, without people shouting my name and bothering me. I didn't answer the lady, but just walked by. I ended up in the park, on a bridge arching over a little, trickling water flowing over the sharp rocks beneath it.

I looked out at the view, and placed my hands on the railing of the bridge, then looked down, to stare at the river below me, the water dancing over the rocks like miniature elves. I even thought I caught a glimpse of a little body sparkling on a stone, but the next second I could see that it just was an old coin shining in the sun.

I couldn't be gay. I just couldn't be. But yet, her kiss had made me feel so alive, made me feel so alive and - and right. I couldn't be gay, or bi – but yet, her kiss had made me love myself for the shortest of moments, and had made me love... her?

*

"Mrs. Smith said she saw you in town today. She even greeted you, but you didn't reply to her..." mom said in a reproaching voice, as she gave me two spoonful mashed potatoes. I repressed the urge to roll my eyes at her, and said in a faked cheerful voice, "Must've missed her. How unfortunate," I did not succeed to repress my disdain. She sent me an annoyed look, and squinted her eyes evilly at me.

"You know how I hate this city mom. I still don't get why we couldn't move to New York or something like that." I said as I shoveled a great mouthful of mashed potatoes into my mouth. She shot me a second, scorned look, clearly not liking the fact that I ate and spoke at the same time.

"Mrs. Smith is pregnant. Mrs. LaCreevy told me last week when I met her on the street. She's your English teacher if I'm not very mistaken?"

I nodded, once again with my mouth full of food. She nodded thoughtfully, and took a mouthful in silence. I watched her eat, and played around with the food on my plate.

I wanted to move away more than ever. Away from all the feelings that had arisen in me, away from everything; that was what I wanted... to get away from everything. Especially pregnant Mrs. Smith

CHAPTER SEVENTEEN

That night I had the nightmare again. Everything was dark and cold, and the dark was eating me up, chewing on me like a dog with its toy. Everything hurt, hurt so terribly, and it was like thousand of hands were touching me, choking me up, tying ropes around my legs and arms, making me unable to move, unable to even scream even though I tried to open my mouth and scream, scream until my lungs gave up and I would die, die in this dark, cold part of my mind, and I couldn't do anything. Nothing could save me now...

And then I woke up with a jerk, jerked out of the world I entered when I dreamt, the evil world that would do anything to kill me. Maybe I awoke because of the scream that flew out of my mouth, maybe it was because of the weight on my blanket, maybe it was because the dawn could be see n outside the window, the sun setting fire to the clouds, maybe it was because of the fact that my phone was playing a melody indicating I had received a text, maybe it was because the curtains of the window was drawn, permitting the light of day to enter my room. I don't know what it was, but the fact of the matter was that I woke up, staring directly into two big brown eyes surrounded by short, black eyelashes. She smiled and leaned forwards until our noses touched and then – then she kissed me; a soft gentle kiss, directly on the lips. For a second or two we were completely still as she gripped my shoulders tightly – but then I jerked away. It was the second time in only a few days I had been kissed by a girl. I knew who it was without thinking over it.

It was Amy, of course it was Amy. She had once again somehow snuck into the house to sit on top of me and making me dream the worst nightmares, letting me drown in the dark, killing me slowly. She pulled a little my long brown hair and smiled gently to me. She looked so innocent, as though she hadn't done anything. I wanted to scream at her. She was the dark; she was the one causing me pain. In this moment I wanted her to die, or dissolve in the air, or at least get away from me. But I needed to talk to her. She had promised she could get the missing piece of me back.

"We need to talk," I said, with a very certain voice. Amy didn't speak at first, just looked at me for a long time, before she finally nodded determined, and reached out for my hand. "Not here. Outside," she said calmly.

She seized my hand although I tried to avoid her grip, and she opened the window and we climbed out, stepped onto the branch of a tree growing just outside my window and glided down the wood. She dragged me along after her as she ran through the city, which seemed much bigger and a little scary in the dark, until we reached the harbor where she pulled me down to the little area with some big stones she ordered me to sit down on. I obeyed.

"Okay, let's talk," she said, with a voice that if anything did not invite for talking. She sounded slightly bored too, and bit her nails carelessly as I stuttering tried to explain myself: "I really need to talk to you, er, because… Ugh, um, because ever since we met, that evening on this very harbor, um…" She sighed irritated, and I could feel her annoyance radiate like the sun. She wanted me to hurry up. To be honest, I wanted to hurry up too, but I didn't know how to get my point across. "Sorry I'm pausing in my speech all the time, but um…" I looked up at the sky where stars were blinking faintly, almost pushed aside of the dawn.

"You see, Amy, ever since I met you, I've been feeling like there's something missing in me… Or maybe I've always missed something, I just didn't realize that before," I said, with a shaky voice. "I think you've got it, that piece of me, I mean. Ever since I met you, I've been feeling so lost and confused." I fumbled shyly with my nails. Amy made me nervous, maybe because I constantly had a feeling something bad would happen when I was around her.

"Except when you were kissing Louisa," she said with a naughty smirk on her lips. "How do you – well it's true, I did feel complete when I kissed her, but how do you know about that kiss?" She ignored my question, and looked at me with her eyebrows raised, as though she expected me to conclude something over that. Knowing Amy like I did, she probably did expect that.

I remembered what my mom had said. "I'm not even positive they're human." Could Amy be some kind of fallen angel; a dark angel, trying to convert me to evil?

She sighed deeply, as though she knew what I thought, and nudged me in the side. "I just know, okay?" Her voice was definitive; there was no chance I could get to know more. I sighed deeply, just like she had done seconds before. "Anyway, is there any chance that you can give me that piece of me back?"

I already knew the answer. I wouldn't get it back just like that, I had to fight for it. "No, you can't." she said gently, and – this was really weird, I thought – patted me on the back, as though trying to make me feel better from a tough breakdown. "I can't give it to you, because I don't have it!" Then who did? Who could save me from the dark? I could feel the tears stinging in my eyes. I just wanted to be normal. I JUST WANTED TO BE NORMAL. NORMAL.

I hid my face in my hands. I suddenly felt so tired and sad. I wanted to sleep forever – but even that, I couldn't do. The nightmares were haunting me. Amy, this fallen angel or whatever supernatural being she could be, was haunting me, and thus causing the nightmares.

"But you can stop the nightmares –" my head shot up from my hands at this, "- and get back yourself if you – if you realize, if you figure out that you're –" she stammered, and suddenly it seemed that she couldn't speak, like her tongue was tied. "I can't say it," she annoyed disclaimed, and hit her forehead in disbelief. "My point is, you can stop it before it goes too far," she murmured into her hand. "How? How do I do that Amy?"

"You just need to make a rope," she said in a voice that seemed to be appropriate when explaining a little child that two plus two is four.

"How do I do that?" I asked uncomfortably, and shifted on the rock.. She sighed deeply, and flicked her hair behind her shoulder. I felt like a two year old, as she said, "Close your eyes and put your hands over your ears when I say so. I'll hold your nose. When you're back in the dark, you imagine a rope of light, which you hold onto. You grasp that rope as tightly as you can, and you follow it." She said, as a matter of fact, as though I should have realized this long ago. "Well, it sounds simple enough…" I said doubtfully, and she nodded.

"You may not succeed the first time," she said, and shot me an apologetic look. "Okay, close your eyes and put your hands over your ears," she commanded.

At first, everything was just plain dark – I couldn't see, hear or smell anything – but slowly, very slowly, the dark slithered into my very skin, and suddenly I was lying in a puddle of pain and dark, and I was hurting so terribly, as my dad's cold voice whispered in my ears although I could not hear anything.

You certainly don't want to your family needs to know your little secret - the voice climbed across my skin, as cold hands which felt after an entrance, a way to my heart; do you? Little Emma won't allow her family to know who she is… I tried to think despite the way the dark pressed against me from all sides.

I tried to scream once again, but once again I couldn't, and I tried to breathe but I couldn't and everything was fuzzy and I felt like the world was spinning although everything was dark, and hands ran up and down my body, slithering up my throat, choking me.

In that very moment I knew I probably would die in the dark – but once again my eyes opened wide and the dark lifted. For a moment I did not know what I was doing, standing there while a girl held my nose closed so I couldn't smell anything, and I didn't understand why I was covering my ears – and then reality crashed onto me. I had failed. Amy knew it too, she understood that I couldn't do it. "I can't do it Amy, I know you said how to – how to do it, but I can't. I just can't, and I won't ever be able to do it."

She didn't argue, although she looked like she wanted to. She just nodded, and helped me get onto my feet again. I swayed lightly in the wind. I felt faint, like I could lose conscious any moment.

We walked the way home in silence, and didn't say anything before we reached the tree I had climbed down from, less than an hour ago. "I'll see you at school today, I suppose," I said as I turned around to say goodbye to her.

"Oh, I don't go to that school," she said with a wide smirk on her lips. She clearly liked messing with my head. "Bye,"

And then she turned around and ran out of my garden. I was left standing there, gaping, staring after her. When I, a few moments later, had collected myself I climbed the tree once again, picked up my backpack and went downstairs to make me some breakfast. After I had ate a bowl of oats and milk I ran out the door with my skateboard under my arm. I needed to be on the edge right now, I needed to figure out what to do. When I reached the school, I knew what I needed to do.

I had to talk to Rochelle.

CHAPTER EIGHTEEN

I found her in the library, surrounded by books and sitting on a couch, alone, reading Harry Potter. Although I could see she sat there, she looked far away, as though Harry Potter had grabbed her and brought her into the fantasy world where dragons existed along with elves, magic, prophecies and – perhaps the most important - love.

But wasn't that what happened when you read a book – you go on a journey with the main characters. When I was younger, I had used to think life was a book, that there was a meaning with everything, a destiny, fate. That things had a meaning. Maybe I was right – maybe I was really just a character in a book, and nothing more. But there wasn't time to philosophize; I had a task to fulfill,

"Rochelle?" I asked hesitantly and the ginger looked up at me. We just looked at each other for a moment, before she grumpily said, "What?" I hadn't expected her to be angry. I fiddled nervously with my shirt and sighed deeply before I said, "Can I talk to you? Alone?"

For a moment it looked like she'd object, but then she nodded, and marked the page in Harry Potter.

She packed away her book and slung her rucksack over her shoulder. She followed me out of the library still without saying a word. We walked quickly through the corridors, and didn't stop before we had reached the outdoor-grounds, and I had dragged her towards the shade of a nearby tree. "I have to talk to you about something," I said, and crossed my arms, although it wasn't that cold. I wanted to put some distance between the two of us, especially because of the questions I wanted to ask her. I felt like an intruder, nosing around in her business... But if she really liked me, if I really was right about this, she was the only one who could help me.

"Rochelle, are you gay?" I asked seriously. For a moment it seemed that she would just laugh it off, but the next moment I could see the tears building up in her eyes. "Why would you think that?" she asked with a shaky voice. "You said you loved me, and I didn't quite believe you when you said it just were a friendly love," I mumbled, pausing every other moment to play with my fingers.

"Yeah, it's true. I like you. But I'm not gay, sorry to disappoint you," she said, a bit harsh. Maybe she was trying to hold back her tears. She was blinking a lot, her eyelashes fluttering up and down, and she was avoiding my gaze, her fingers playing with the hem of her shirt.

"But if you're not gay, how can you like me..?" I asked confused, "Are you bisexual?" She shook her head in disagreement. "I'm pan -" a loud sniffle and then -"pansexual." I raised my eyebrows in confusion. What did pans have to do with anything? "You're pan-sexual? What's, uh, what's that?" I asked, questioning her sanity. Was she sexually attracted to pans? Or was it just another label for gay? Was she just trying to avoid calling herself gay?

She sat down, and leaned her back against the tree, still playing with her shirt, wrapping the textile around her finger and exhaled loudly, almost a yawn. She was making fun of me, because I didn't understand her. Because I didn't get it. "Pan-sexuality is not about being sexually attracted to pans. It's about loving hearts, not parts. I can fall in love with anyone. A boy, a girl, non-binary, I don't see a gender. I'm gender-blind, meaning that I see their gender, but it doesn't make them less or more attractive to me. I could fall in love with a trans-gender person. Trans-gender means you don't fit into a two gender binary. You don't identify with the gender you were assigned at birth. For example, if you were born a girl, you want to be a boy, or vice versa. Sometimes you don't even identify with either of them, or maybe you identify with both of them. Pan-sexuality is about loving hearts, not parts."

She finished her little speech with another loud sigh, and started fiddling around with her nails, cleaning them. "So... you're attracted to everyone?" I asked. In the second the words had left my mouth, I knew I was being ignorant."No, I still care about who they are as a person; it's just that their gender and sexual identity has nothing to do with that." She explained softly.

"But how did you know that you're pan?" I asked, pressuring her to speak. The girl with the red hair nodded slightly. "Yeah, how did I know I'm pan...? I guess I just thought about my experiences in attraction, what I wanted and what I desired, and I realized that I don't care what gender my significant other is." She said, and then – my eyes widened in shock at this – she took my hand, intertwined our fingers and ran her thumb over my skin. It calmed me down, made me relax a little. I didn't remove my hand from her grip. I just sat there, thinking. She had figured out her sexuality out by thinking. Perhaps I could do that too? Perhaps I, if I thought enough about it, would realize that I was completely normal, and go on with my life. Perhaps I could live without that missing piece, live without Amy's 'help'... But I knew that I wouldn't be able to do it. I had to be fulfilled again. Just like I had been when I kissed –

I withdrew my hand, and stood up angrily. "You know that - I don't like you like that, you know that right?" I said, stammering and spluttering, trying to explain why I hadn't just removed my hand from hers, or maybe I was explaining why I had let her hold it... I did not know why I had done either of those things. I got to my feet, and reached out a hand for her to take. She did not accept the offer, but got up herself, slung her rucksack over one shoulder once again, and walked away. And I was left alone, deep in thought.

Chapter Nineteen

I spent the last few minutes in the library, hiding behind the shelves filled with books, reading the backside of the books that looked interesting, and found a few that I would like to read. I couldn't deal with my classmates right now, so I'd gladly risk to be delayed to English instead of spending the last few minutes in the company of Rochelle, Sophia or Lee, and that other girl, whose name I could not remember. But it wasn't just a desire to read that brought me to the library, avoiding Lee, Sophia and especially Rochelle. I needed to think, and the best place to do that was when I was accompanied by the best friends I had ever known – books. I opened numerous books at random, and looked at the pages, hoping for some guideline to show up between the lines about magic, dragons, drugs and complications. I wanted advice, absolutely, but moreover I wanted to feel like I wasn't alone. I wasn't even really sure what it was I felt alone over. I just knew I was different somehow. I didn't really fit in, not anymore anyway, if I ever had.

I pulled out my phone, unlocked it, and clicked around on it. I had no new messages on Facebook, and I felt stupid for even thinking I would've got one. I had hoped Louisa would be interested in knowing why I had run off like that when we kissed; and at the same time, I was terrified that she'd ask me why I had ran for it. But then again, it probably was quite obvious to her. I hadn't liked the kiss. At least that was what she was bound to think. The truth was that I had loved that kiss. I had replayed it over and over in my mind as I had looked on the pages in books without really seeing the words, because the thought of her scent of lip-balm and the feeling of her deliciously soft skin beneath my hand was haunting me. I sat down tiredly. I just felt so very tired, as I held a book and a phone in my hands. And I fell asleep – I must've; all I knew was, that suddenly I was back in the dark, fingers creeping onto my skin, the dark seeping into my very chore.

And then I bolted up. I inhaled the almost liquefied air sharply when I felt it; it was probably what had caused me to wake up in the first place– something wet on my forehead. I sat up quickly, pushed the wet something away, and opened my mouth to scream, but no words came out. Instead I could feel the tears well up in my eyes, and roll out, one by one, slowing falling into my still open mouth and my nose. I tried to dry them away, but there just kept coming more of them, slowly falling. It was stupid, it was ridiculous, but I couldn't stop crying.

Finally I managed to look up – and of course, there she was. Amy, holding a wet cloth in her hand that she'd obviously just used to put on my sweaty forehead to cool me down. I squinted at her. This didn't make sense. Amy never had helped me before – she always said she was trying to help me, but she only destroyed me. Why would she participate in something so lovingly as drying the sweat of my face? She smiled softly at me, and then, out of a sudden – she disappeared. I didn't get to see where she had run off to; one moment she was there, the next she was gone.

The bell started ringing as I stood there, with a book in one hand and my phone in the other, scrolling through my Facebook news feed, hoping for a message that never would arrive. I quickly pressed the book back onto the shelf between two other books, not caring about the alphabetic order, and ran out of the library, running into other people every other moment, and stepping on quite a few toes on the students that were on their way up to the library with their teachers. An entire class was filling almost the whole corridor, and I had a pretty hard time running through the crowd without making anybody. I needed to hurry a lot – this next lesson was with Mrs. LaCreepy, sorry, LaCreevy, and it was no joke to do something like that in her vicinity, just like making fun of her name would earn you a detention. She wasn't like the French teacher, Mr. Babin, who let one do whatever one wanted to do in his lessons as long as you were able to ask to go to the toilet in French. I finally skipped to a halt, and retraced my steps once – I had run past the door to our classroom. Perhaps I would be lucky, and it would turn out that Mrs. LaCreepy was late, or sick or for some reason couldn't teach today – please just let today be the day she's not here, I thought desperately, as I opened the door.

Of course things did not actually turn out the way I wished. Boney Mrs. LaCreepy was standing in front of the blackboard, and with a piercing stare she made me squirm under her gaze. With an ever so soft voice, she calmly said, "I'm disappointed in you," – it definitely also sounded like that. She sounded like I had just betrayed her, sold her soul to the devil or something, not just arrived late at a lesson. "Let's see if a detention could improve your ability to be on time next time, shall we, Miss. Oaksby?" I just nodded distantly, and jogged to my seat at the front, beside Miss. Adams, whose first name I did not care for. I quickly found my books and my pencil case, from which I found a pencil and an eraser. Finally I got my notebook and opened it on an empty page. I did all this without looking at anybody. I did not want to by mistake cast a glance at Rochelle or the others; honestly I did not even want to look at the girl sitting beside me. I just wanted to be left alone, wanted everyone to ignore me, which was very unlike me. Usually I wanted all the attention I could possibly get, practicing tricks on my skateboard to seem cooler, and make people notice me… but not today. Today I wanted to be alone.

"As I was saying before we were interrupted," Mrs. LaCreepy said, shooting me a nasty glare before she turned around to write on the blackboard with a screeching piece of chalk, "what did the author mean when he talks about 'like snakes under the skin'," she wrote the quote on the board and turned. I allowed myself to drift away, letting Mrs. LaCreepy's voice become a soft background noise as I hid my face in my hands. So Rochelle "the Rock" Stewarts were pansexual. And she liked me. She wasn't even afraid to admit it, when I flat out had asked her. The label fit her. Hearts, not parts. She fell in love purely based on the personality of the other person. That was pretty beautiful; even I had to admit that. Could that be what I was? That would definitely explain my feelings for – no, I couldn't be. I was not into girls – at all. I remembered a quote I once had seen on a website of funny memes. A blonde, pretty girl looking troubled as she says, "I don't even like looking at my own vagina." It was from a show, a show about lesbians. I hadn't watched it, of course nor, since I was not into girls at all. Except that I was.

"Miss Oaksby? Miss Oaksby!" I was brutally being pulled back into reality, where Mrs. LaCreepy was staring at me with a nasty look in her eyes. If she hadn't already given me a detention as punishment, she'd no doubt have given me one now. "We were talking about the blue curtains," she said, pointing the chalk in her hands at me.

"Oh… Um, s-sorry. I suspect the curtains which are blue… because… I think they are, er, a symbol of his eternal depression." I said hesitantly, glancing down at the text in my book which I had read yesterday. I thanked a higher power for that in this moment, as I sat there, trying to regulate the heat in my body. I was sure my head was flushed. I could feel the blood rushing to my cheeks as I looked down at the textbook.

"Hm… very good. By the way, you meet me at three o'clock at this classroom where you will serve your punishment." She said with a determined voice. There was no way I could convince her to change her mind and let me go after last lesson like the rest of the class. But whatever, I thought, slightly grumpily. At least I'd not get time to meet Amy or anything like that, if I was delayed at school. We had not made a deal of when we would meet next time, but I was determined to avoid meeting her at all. She was scary, and she did scary things to me.

At three o'clock I was standing outside the door, and knocked twice on it, before I entered the classroom. Mrs. LaCreepy – LaCreevy – was sitting behind her desk, a pair of glasses balancing on the tip of her nose. She looked up briefly. "I've been waiting for somebody to clean up the room properly. You will do just that." She said, and pointed to a bucket full of water standing on a table in the back of the class. I walked to it, and dipped my hands in the warm water, searching for the cloth that was swimming in the water. I got a chair and started to clean up the top of the lamps on the ceiling. I worked slowly. Mrs. LaCreepy hadn't said how long I would have to work, but I was pretty sure the school only could keep a student there till four o'clock. If I had to do this work, I'd rather do it properly. When I returned to the table with the bucket, I saw a slip of paper: that had definitely not been there a few minutes ago. Strange. I hadn't seen anyone in the room beside Mrs. LaCreepy, and she hadn't moved from her paperwork for as much as a second, other than to sip from a cup of coffee. I quickly looked up to check whether she was looking at me, before I looked at the little slip of paper. It looked as though somebody had scribbled the message very fast, as though they did not have time to form the letters properly. It said, "I'm getting you out of here. –Amy."

Amy? Amy was getting me out of her? And more importantly – how the fuck had she managed to sneak a message on a piece of paper into the room without anyone noticing – without me noticing. I decided to ignore the message, and continued to work on the lamps. The minutes ticked by slowly, and then – without warning – somebody thrust open the door, and jumped into the room. "Come Emma, we're leaving now," a familiar voice said determined, and a hand reached out to grab mine. Amy took my hand, and we turned to leave the room (I was stunned, and was just following the trail), when, at that moment, Mrs. LaCreepy coughed loudly. I had expected this, and turned around again. "We can't hang out now Amy, I've got detention as you can see," I said calmly, slightly relieved to be honest, and ran toward the bucket once again. "No," Amy said. "I can explain, Mrs." She said to Mrs. LaCreevy, and looked directly at her. LaCreevy didn't say anything, just sat there, staring stunned at her. Another strange thing about this whole strange situation was also that although

Amy had said she'd explain, not a word fell from her lips. She just stood there, staring at my teacher. LaCreevy blinked hesitantly a couple times, and then she said, "You're right. She can leave,"

Incredulously I stared at the two women before me, before Amy took my hand, and literally dragged me out of the room. I had to almost run to keep up with her. I maybe could've escaped from her, but I was too stunned to think about doing anything, let alone walk away. I was simply too stunned over what just had happened, and what it meant. Amy had shown me just how powerful she was.

Chapter Twenty

She barged open the door to the entrance, and we ran out onto the small road made of bricks, leading us out of the school. She clenched my hand so tight it hurts, but I didn't mind. I didn't mind because it suddenly felt like the first time I had met her. I felt free, as I half walked, half ran beside her.

"What are you doing?" I asked breathlessly, trying to be angry at her, but failing miserably. I just couldn't hate her right now. I knew she was some kind of angel, and she was just trying to help me, although her help was pretty poor. "I've got detention, I'm supposed to be at the school," I said, almost hiccupping up the words as I stumbled on behind her as she dragged me on. "Do you really want to clean up that classroom?" Amy asked with a chuckle, and shook her head in response to herself. "We've got work to do. A lot of it." She said with another shake of her head, like she was giving up on me, like I was an impossible case. I felt a little pang in my chest, as I felt taken aback, but I didn't want to ruin this moment. "What're we going to do?" I asked, excited like a little girl as I skipped along with her on the brick floor. "We're going to help you," she said with a determined voice, and pulled at my hand to get me to hurry up.

"How did you even deliver that message?" I asked her. Her only response was another pull at my arm. She wasn't going to answer, I knew it. Then I was just going to figure it out on my own, I thought. I decided to give asking her another go. "How did you place that slip of paper on the table without me noticing?" I asked, having made the decision to solve this mystery. Against any expectation I had, Amy replied.

"Why should I tell you that?" Her voice was shaking, perhaps with anger, or perhaps with fear; fear that I would figure her out and not find her as interesting as she seemed to me right now. There was no chance of that. I could recognize a unique person when I saw one, and that was just what she was. Unique. Maybe that was what made her so scary – because she was one of the only real things in a terribly fake world. She was an angel, fallen or on a mission for the good lord above… I was suddenly jerked out of my thoughts as she came to a halt, and I bumped into her. We had reached a traffic sign, and were waiting for the lights to turn green. Finally it did, and we continued walking. I picked up the thread of thoughts at where I had left it. Who was Amy, really? Wasn't it appropriate that I could get to know that, when Amy seemingly knew my secrets? She had known about the nightmares, she'd known about the kiss, and God knows what else she knew about me.

"Who are you Amy?" I asked aggressively, and tried to pull my hand from hers. She just clenched it even tighter, until I gave up. She'd probably stopped the blood circulation in it. "Later." She said shortly, and dragged me down a little road that ended at the harbor, where she placed me at a big rock that I recognized from the night we'd met for the first time.

"Now I can address your questions," she said softly, and kneeled in front of me, taking my hands, gently holding them in hers, entwining her fingers with mine.

"You want to know who I am, huh?" she said with a voice which quivered slightly; not a lot, but there was an unmistakable tremble in it. I nodded, and repeated my question softly.

"Who are you, Amy?"

"You can call me Lololi. There is always love." She replied to her knees as she looked down. "You can call me Ashika. Passionate lover. You can call me Widad. Love. You can call me anything you want. I'm Amy."

"What's your last name Amy?" I was whispering the words.

She raised her head slowly, and looked me into my eyes. "You already know."

"No, I don't. You have to tell me. I need to know. I really, really need to know. You're supposed to help me, why don't you actually do that?"

"If I could help you just by telling you everything, I'd do it, but I can't. You wouldn't believe me either. You have to figure it out by yourself," she replied calmly

"And I want to know how you sent me that message," I said with a voice that – I was surprised – did not waver in the slightest, as I changed the topic.

"I can't tell you that. I'm sorry, but it's against the rules. I can't tell you everything, only the basics. You might hate me for it, but please believe me when I say that I'm sorry," she said gently, and ran her thumb over my hand. It felt comforting. For the second time that day, I felt like crying. My eyes were stinging dangerously, and I could feel them well up. I looked upwards to keep the tears in. The sky was blue, September blue as I called it; the kind of blue sky you only see in September. Was that Amy's home? The sky? Was she sent out from 'the good Lord above'? Somehow it didn't seem realistic. But where was she from then, this angel that for some reason was trying to help me, according to what mom said... But in reality it seemed more like she was trying to kill me slowly. Why did I trust her then? I didn't understand anything.

Then I remembered what my mom had said, once again thinking the words in my mind. She wasn't sure they were human, these helpers, as they were too beautiful and angelic... I blinked – I had remembered! There was one thing I had to ask Amy. "Why aren't you a boy Amy? Mom said these helpers are supposed to be the opposite sex." I looked down at her once again, my urge to cry no longer pressing me to look away. It was like they had vanished as the thought of why Amy wasn't a boy had entered my brain. It was an important question; I could feel it in every fiber of my body. I needed an answer to this, almost as much as I needed oxygen to breathe and be alive. Only when I'd solved this mystery the nightmares would stop; only then would

I be fulfilled, only then would I get back the missing piece of me, that I had lost somewhere.

She shook her head and sighed. "I hate this. I want to tell you everything, but you have got to figure it out by yourself..." she said. For a moment she looked hesitantly at me with her big, pretty eyes, and her brown hair flowing lightly in the wind. "But... I could give you a hint," she said as she withdrew her hands and started to twirl the edge of her her blouse in her hands. It struck me that she probably was getting stiff in the entire body too, as she kneeled, "Come sit beside me," I said softly, and took her hand again, tugging slightly at her.

She got to her feet and sat down beside me. "It's about... Feelings. And girls." She said gently and once again she took my hand, playing with my fingers. "That's really all I can say I think..." she said, trailing off at the end of the sentence, and squeezed my hand tightly.

"Now come on, we've got a lot of work to do."

I didn't even need to ask her what we were going to do; I already knew. I clenched my eyes shut and placed my hands over my ears as she leaned forwards and clenched my nose so I couldn't smell anything.

When I closed my eyes and ears, the dark came instantly. I wondered for a second, trying to count the times I had been left alone in the dark the last 24 hours. I wasn't sure if it was two or three times, maybe even more. Everything was blurred and fuzzy – but then I could no longer think, as dark hands creeped over my skin, tickling me in a dangerous way. A tickle that said; I'm trying to make you laugh before I kill you. It'd kill me, this dark. The dark of the lonely, tortured souls.

Chapter Twenty One

For the first time in all that time I had spent in the dark, I found that I could scream. I could open my mouth without being suffocated. That wasn't the only thing that had changed though. It was like the ropes of dark that was surrounding my body was looser. Like they weren't knotted as tightly around me anymore. Like I was winning over the dark. I knew it was stupid to get my hopes up as I panicked (although I wasn't tied as tightly as I usually was, the dark was enough to scare me shitless) opened my mouth and screamed, screamed until there was no air back in my lungs and my heart was pounding and I couldn't get away from the dark, tickling my body with soft movements, cradling me softly like water at the ocean. It felt as though I was lying on the shore of a beach and the water was closing above my head. I couldn't get up, I couldn't breathe, I couldn't swim away, because this was just dark, and it was horrible. I did not know what to do… Then, suddenly, Amy's words echoed in my head. "Make a rope."

I just had to make a rope out of the darkness, and grip it tightly, following it until I could see the light. It seemed rather pointless; there were dark all the way around me, but I decided that it was the best plan I had. It was the only plan I had got. I imagined a thin rope made out of nothing; a rope as thin as the hairs on a toothbrush, but a rope nonetheless. And slowly, ever so slowly, I could feel it materializing in my hand. It happened slowly, then all at once; one moment my hands were empty, the next moment a tickling feeling spread over my outstretched hand, and I could feel it appear in my palm. A thin, very fragile rope. I pushed myself up to my knees (I did only just now realize I was lying down) and clenched the string in my hand, my nails pressing into the flesh of my skin. I inhaled air sharply and started walking. Constantly I was tickled on my entire body, like feathers was surrounding me, clashing against my skin. I didn't feel safe. Although I'd been able to get to my feet without as much as removing the ropes tied around me, although there happened nothing right now, here in the dead silence, I was scared. The dark was scary, no matter how often I was there, no matter what I did. But perhaps I was not only scared; maybe I was also a little hopeful. If I had been able to make a rope, I might as well also be able to stop the dark fully and completely.

I walked in complete silence; it was like my accomplishment had glued my lips together in awe over what I had done. I walked and walked, but I wasn't sure I moved at all. I was tickled by invisible feathers every moment, but I had no other indicator that I really was moving. I just walked and walked, in the blinding dark. Blind and deaf I walked with my hand wrapped around the string of rope, the string that was the best hope I had. A thought struck me. If I could make a rope out of mere thoughts, then I could probably also make it glow in the dark. I wanted a little light; this dark was scary and uncomfortable. I closed my eyes (or at least, I thought I did, because there was absolutely no change of lightning) and wished for light. Let the rope glow, I thought firmly, and to my delight, it actually happened. It wasn't much; just a faint glow, a dim light issuing from the thin string in my hand. The strange thing was… It didn't make the dark disappear. It illuminated it. I reached out in wonder, and ran my fingers over the surface of… feathers? It really was feathers. The dim light illuminated the feathers around me. They were formed in a soft curve around me, all the time close to my body. That was what had tickled me – feathers. It probably was the same thing I had felt when I thought fingers were creeping over my skin. My face split in a wide smile.

And just like that, I was jerked back to reality as my blue eyes flew up, and I let out a small whimper. I did not know why; but it felt like I had lost something very valuable, something very important, and I felt like I'd never get it back. I had understood the dark, I had almost had control over it, but then I had been pulled back to this world. In front of me Amy was sitting on her knees, once again. She'd apparently moved down in front of me instead of beside me. It felt more intimate this was. I looked at her and shook my head. "I'm sorry, I couldn't do it," I said and smiled weakly. She took my hand and squeezed it gently. "You were almost there," she said, and sounded somewhat proud. I wasn't sure though; I could not see anything to be proud over myself. I'd only be filled with pride when I had stopped these nightmares. "But Amy, I didn't do it. Why is it so important that I almost did it? It's useless. An almost is not good enough, can't you see?" I asked, and hid my face in my hands.

"And another thing… I feel like I can't live without the dark, now that I've lived with it for so long, and have seen the feathers," I mumbled into my fingers, but it seemed like she heard me. She was silent for a few seconds before she said: "You don't have to live without it. You have to learn how to live with it, co-exist. Next time you go back into the dark, it'll be perhaps even scarier than it normally is, because you've discovered the feathers, but I promise you… It'll be worth it in the end. I know that."

"Yeah, perhaps that's true. But I'm not going anywhere right now." I said firmly, and played with her fingers to avoid looking into her eyes.

"You have to go back!" she said, sounding slightly panicked and disturbed. I just shook my head. I couldn't take going back into the darkest corners of my mind. I refused to take that quest right now. I did not want to get lost in the dark again.

"It can show you who you are!" she said persistently, as she ran a hand through my hair and tucked a strand of my brown hair back behind my ear.

"You have to go back." She said once again. Have to? I don't have to do anything.

"I'm not special at all, how am I supposed to fight against something like that?" I cried out. I could feel my eyes turning watery once again. I looked up at the sky, just like I had done earlier, to keep my tears in. I didn't want to seem weak, not to her. I wanted to look strong, like I was able to do anything I set my mind to. I wanted to be that girl who had all her shit in order. But I wasn't that girl. I looked down again, and gazed at the pretty girl sitting beside me

"You're right, you're not special, if you mean that as in you are 'better' –" she made quotation marks in the air, "- than the next person. No one is better than anyone else." She said. "But you're unique."

"I can't save the world!" I screamed into her face, screamed it into her open eyes, like needles trying to stab her, blind her, and disarm her, her and her stupid words about fighting. Out of a sudden it once again felt like she was the enemy. How could I have been so blind? She wasn't trying to help me. She was trying to kill me, slowly.

"You're not saving the world. You're saving yourself." She replied in a whisper, her eyes saying sorry to me, as she pushed me back, back into the corners of my mind that I had never explored myself, simply out of fear. She wasn't the enemy. My own worst enemy was myself.

CHAPTER TWENTY TWO

I didn't need to close my eyes this time. The dark came without warning as Amy prodded me on my shoulder, and reality flew out of reach. And I was back in the dark.

You already know what you are... don't you, abomination? The voice was silky, but sharp. Like a sword, cutting my thoughts from my brain, cutting me. Making me a simple silhouette of who I was supposed to be, cutting off my personality, cutting me away from the Nirvana songs I listened to on Sunday mornings, cutting off the constellations of stars that I wanted to see, cutting me away from everything. My dad's voice, as he tried to kill me slowly, suffocating me in a pillow of soft feathers.

You certainly don't want to your family needs to know your little secret - the voice climbed across my skin, as cold hands which felt after an entrance, a way to my heart; do you? Little Emma won't allow her family to know who she is...

I nodded slightly. No, I could not let my family know about this, I could not let them know me. I could not draw up the strength to imagine up a rope of hope; I was empty and cold. I could not hope anymore. I did not have any power left in my entire body, and I let everything go limp, and my senses went numb as I closed my eyes and thought of Louisa, and how I never had said sorry for leaving after that kiss, and I thought about how I regretted leaving her, though I had loved the kiss and hated her for it.. And then... Then something strange happened.

I could feel warmth spreading throughout my body – starting in my feet, warming, travelling upwards, growing hotter and hotter as the spot where my knees was buckled up from the heat, broke; it felt as if I was made of glass and I was shattering into pieces. But I was picking myself up from the ground, collecting the pieces up, trying to fit them together. I thought of the taste of lime lip balm and soft skin, and I broke even more and collected myself and fitting the pieces together in new and unknown ways as I slowly felt myself rising from the ground; I didn't stand on my feet, no, I was rising higher than that. Higher, higher, and the dark turned lighter and lighter as something moved on my shoulder blades as I rose.

I was rising; I was flying.

I had wings; they were moving behind me. I was a dark angel, the dark spreading behind me in thousands of dark feathers. It wasn't Amy who was a fallen angel – or maybe she was, but I was too.

I had been scared of my own wings. I had been scared of the heights I could rise to. I'd been scared, and I understood everything now. Everything fit together like a puzzle. I understood. I understand. I had wanted attention for everything I wasn't. But now I didn't need attention – because I was simply me. I was simply me, and I was flying. Softly my wings carried me through the air – my surroundings were white, light and bright, so bright in almost hurt my eyes. I flew through the air, until I softly was sat on the ground and my wings folded back onto my back. In that very moment, I opened my eyes. I was positioned on the rock I had left such a short time ago, although it felt like a lifetime. My wings were gone – but that was okay. They'd always be there if I needed them. And in front of me, Amy was sitting, holding my hands so I sat up instead of rolling off the rock, when I had... lost consciousness, or whatever it was that happened when I closed my eyes and found myself in the dark.

"Do you know who you are now?" she asked, playing with a lock of my hair as I removed my hands from her grasp. I inhaled her scent sharply; I could smell vanilla in the air. So that was what an angel smelled like. It was beautiful, that smell. "I think so," I said. "I flew. I really flew..." I couldn't quite comprehend that it really had happened. I had flown by the help of my wings. I tried to touch my shoulder-blades to check if there was any sign of the wings, but there was not as much as a bump or a wound after them. Did that mean they'd never been there? No, it didn't. They'd been there, in the reality I'd been in.

"Yes, you did. I'm so proud of you," she said contently, and tried to hug me lovingly, obviously only with good intentions, but I pushed her arms away. "I need to think for a while," I said gently, as I got to my feet. She looked as though she wanted to protest, but didn't do it, which I was relieved over. I walked away slowly, trying to process what just had happened. Whenever I blinked, I could feel the wings on my back, and I knew they'd always be there to help me fly away in my mind. I could always escape the cruel world I lived in.

I was walking down the street a couple streets away from the park, when somebody shouted my name. "Emma! Emma!" I looked up; it was Mrs. Smith, watering her garden flowers with a can. "Hello Mrs. Smith!" I called, and walked over to the garden fence.

"How's your mom? How's it going at the new school – gosh, I have so much I want to ask you and tell you about! Would you fancy a cup of tea and a biscuit?" she asked happily as she watered her lilies. "Yeah, sure," I replied, and entered the well-groomed garden and followed her through the open door to her house.

She gave me a cup of tea with honey and milk, we sat in her kitchen, and she told me so much, told me about her winter holiday, how she'd been skiing in France, and she told me about the baby mom had told me that she was about to have in seven months – her stomach was bigger than what it used to be – and about how her husband had complained over the bus drivers' attitude towards costumers on the bus: "And then he goes, 'excuse me, I'm the costumer, and I'm asking you to –" I interrupted her in the middle of her sentence.

"Mrs. Smith... can I ask you a question?" I asked nervously, and chewed on a nail.

"Sure thing little one," she said kindly, and drank from her cup. "Do you know anything about... angelic helpers?"

I did not need to say more, the second I had finished my sentence, I understood that she knew exactly what I was talking about. She sat up straight, and put down the cup to signalize that she was alert. I smiled hesitantly at her. She smiled warmly back. "I assume you've already met yours," she said questioningly and raised her eyebrows at me. I just nodded. "yes, yes I have, and I have a question about them, that I couldn't really ask my mom…" I said, trailing off at the end of the sentence. She smiled encouragingly at me, and nodded to let me know that I could continue.

"Have you ever heard about it being a girl when you're a girl? I mean, say, I met my helper, and it was a girl, could that be possible? And why would it happen?" I asked, trying to keep my voice calm, as I sipped at the cup of tea. "It is possible." She said gently, and poured a little more milk into her cup, before she put it to her lips. "I have a friend who experienced that. I also know why it happens." She said in a low voice. At these words I could not keep calm. I gasped as I sipped at the tea and the liquor burned my throat. I didn't give it much thought though; I set down the glass and whispered, "Why? Why does that happen?"

Mrs. Smith smiled at me, clearly noticing how eager I was. "You only meet helpers of the sex you're attracted to," she said, as though that was a matter of fact, something everyone knew, "What do you mean?" I asked, as my stomach gave an unpleasant lurch.

"The girls who has a girl as helper… they're gay Emma. They're attracted to other girls. Girls that meet a boy are heterosexual. I don't know if you get two helpers if you're attracted to both boys and girls, bisexuality, but- what're you doing young lady?" she asked, clearly astonished at my strange behavior –for I had just got to my feet and was pacing back and forth beside the table, going in circles. "Of course," I said, and sighed deeply. "I was right. I was right. You're right Mrs. Smith, thank you so much." I said eagerly, and felt a strong urge to hug her, clench her tightly and cradle back and forth. I smiled widely. Suddenly the old lady seemed like the best person in the world.

"Not to be rude, but I really got to go. I've got loads of homework, and lots of plans for today. But thank you so much, you're the best, you really are," I said, and carried my cup to the sink where I cleaned it up, and then walked back to the hallway where my jacket and my shoes were placed beside the door. She followed me out, clearly astonished, but not trying to hold me back.

She put her arms around me when I had gotten on my jacket and tied my Converses and was standing up straight to say goodbye. She held me tightly, squeezing me lightly and rubbing her hand over my back. "Take care of yourself," she said gently.

"I will," I promised.

*

I walked through the park on my way home, and eventually ended up on the same bridge as a few days ago, watching the water flow over the stones, and thought about how Amy was a girl, and how I felt about Louisa and how her lips had tasted so sweet; I couldn't help it – I replayed the kiss once again, and again, and again. I kept doing it, until I understood, until I knew.

I took a deep breath, and whispered, "I'm gay."

And I was okay with that.

Chapter Twenty Three

What if the missing piece hadn't been a missing piece at all? What if the missing piece was the piece of my soul, which I'd always been ashamed of? What if the missing piece was the part of me that I'd never dared to show anyone? What if that was the piece of me that gave my name meaning – the piece that made me whole...

What if I was just like a butterfly, which had its own wings pinned to the wall, never showing off the beauty of them? What if I was meant to fly, show off my beauty, just like the other butterflies? What if Amy had tried to make me realize that?

I don't know how long I was standing on that bridge, thinking about all those things, understanding how I'd never lost a piece of me – I'd just been afraid of the person I might be. But there was nothing to be afraid of, absolutely nothing. I knew now. I liked girls, and that was perfectly okay. Amy wasn't evil, and neither was the dark. There was no villain in my story, except for the fear that had had me pinned down, had made me unable to move. Now I could move, now I could fly, as a dark angel, soaring through the skies. Amy was an angel or some other supernatural being, and she cared for me. No wonder I felt free when I was with her. She wasn't like Annabelle, who was childish and stupid... and amazing. I'd never forget what those two girls had done for me; one who helped me realize who I was, and one who'd love me for who I was. Not to mention Louisa, the person who'd helped me figure out who I loved. I loved her. I had fallen for her, and I had kissed her, and it had been beautiful, and I could not have asked for anything better in a first kiss.

My thoughts were becoming fuzzy from happiness, like I was drunk on happiness. I couldn't think properly; my thoughts were going in circles, from Amy to Annabelle to Louisa and Amy again. I inhaled the cold fall air through my nose, Yes, I was gay. Gayer than a fucking rainbow, and I did not care about what anyone would think of me, I did not care if anyone treated me differently because of it. I stopped for a moment, and turned the idea over in my head. Did I really not care what people might think of me? No, I was lying to myself if I was saying that I didn't care (and I had lied plenty to myself about my sexuality, I did not need to lie anymore), I cared way too much. And with that realization I crashed down all the way from cloud nine, crashing from the high. And there was no angel to catch me, Amy wasn't around, and she couldn't help me pick up the shattered pieces of me. I was broken once again.

How was I ever going to come out?

*

When you know something nobody else knows, you feel the weight of the world on your shoulders. It's your responsibility to never let anyone know, ever. You've got to fight for the secret to stay a secret.

And when you so desperately want people to know this something, this secret, when you want that as much as I wanted, you start to do anything to make them notice it. The thing was; I also needed to hide it. No one could know – oh, but how I longed for them to know, how I wished and hoped, dreamt of it.

I wanted to come out, but at the same time I really did not want to come out. I wanted people to know who I was, but I was scared. This was such an important part of who I was, that I could not risk that people would hate it, hate me. Who I was, was directly aligned with who I loved. I could not risk telling people that I was gay, and then have them hate me. I just couldn't do it. I spent the next couple of days moping over it in my room, trying to hide it from my mom. At school I hid myself in the library, looking at books and studying. I studied a lot; it was like doing math made my brain stop pressuring me to jump onto a table and scream out that I was gay and always would be; it took every ounce in my body to not run to Louisa's house and apologize to her and tell her the truth… But I couldn't risk it, I just couldn't.

One day in the library, I decided that I was done sneaking around about my feelings for Louisa. I hadn't seen Amy in days, and I was wondering if she'd returned home to wherever she came from, so I couldn't get any help from her. I had also a feeling in my stomach that said that she wanted me to solve this by myself, figure out what to do myself. So that day, a Thursday at the end of the month September, I decided to send her a text. I didn't want to seem clingy, but I didn't want to sound too careless either. I had to hit it right up in that text. I needed to keep it short and simple, but yet effective.

I found my mobile phone in the back pocket of my blue, worn-down jeans. 'Hey Louisa. Want to meet up?'

I closed my eyes a few moments, and thought it over again. There was only one thing left; a few words that I wanted to ask her. I wrote the letters quickly, almost not daring to re-think it while I wrote them, and finally hit send. 'So I can kiss you?'

Oh no, fuck, fuck, fuck. Why did I do that? Stupid, it was the worst idea I'd ever had. I couldn't fix this in a fucking text. Fuck, fuck, fucking hell, how very fucking stupid I was. I exasperated ran a hand through my brown locks of hair, and sighed deeply. I slammed the phone onto a table, and sat down on the couch with my head in my hands. Fuck. That was the worst thing I could've done. I was so stupid, so darn stupid. I could hear the phone buzz on the table. It felt like somebody had turned my guts inside out, when I reached out for it. But it wasn't a rejection or a text about how ridiculous I was, it wasn't a text that stated that she hated me, and never would be able to look at me normally, now that she knew that I was a freak, a fucking lesbo. It wasn't any of those things; it was something much scarier.

'I thought you'd never ask.'

My stomach twisted uncomfortably. I had fallen for this girl.

CHAPTER TWENTY FOUR

I didn't really know how to deal with Louisa's text; I didn't want to seem desperate or anything, so I just ended up not replying to it until I knew what to do to deal with the situation. I tried to ignore it the whole day, but every time I felt my phone in my back-pocket, I thought of how Louisa most likely wanted to kiss me, or at least didn't have anything against me wanting to. She didn't seem to think I just was a freaking 'lesbo'. More than once, I picked up my phone and checked my messages just to see those few words that rang so beautifully in my ears. 'I thought you'd never ask.'

Did this mean that she liked me back? Did it mean that she'd liked our kiss, and wanted to do it again? Was she sexually attracted to me, but not emotionally? Every time I reached this point in my trail of thoughts, I closed my eyes and said a little prayer in my head; "Dear God: I know you're probably busy, but could you please let Louisa be in love with my, just like I am with her. Thank you if you help me, and thanks for being such a kick-ass God who gives us pretty things like flowers and butterflies, and dangerous, wild things like crocodiles. Thank you. Amen."

It was a rather silly prayer, but I had a feeling God wanted Life to be appreciated. Especially the things we humans hadn't destroyed fully, like the scary, wild animals in the jungle. I wanted to give God credit for this world, if there even was a God. I wasn't sure I believed in a man sitting on the clouds, keeping an eye on every single little thing happening down on the Earth. Some religious people said, that homosexuality was a sin according to God's words in the bible. But why should He (or She) care about people's safe and consensual choices?

Maybe I just wanted to believe in an accepting, loving God, perhaps especially a lot more since my realization yesterday. I was gay. Did God make me this way? I didn't know. I didn't even know whether there really was a God or not.

I spent most of my time in school absentmindedly thinking about everything but the homework I should be doing. More specifically was I thinking about the topic of coming out. How was I ever going to be able to tell my family the truth about who I was?

When we got onto computers in our English class, I took my headphones and connected them to the computer, before I typed in the search bar, "lesbian coming out story". As I distractedly did the tasks I listened to a bunch of coming out stories, and I didn't feel as lonely now. I felt less like a freak; other girls had realized that they were lesbian too. It wasn't the end of the world that I had realized that as well. Actually I was lucky I'd realized this early in my life. I was happy I knew that I liked girls this early in my life; but there was someone I wanted to share my happiness with - two persons to be exact. The obvious one was Louisa; the girl I had fallen in love with, the girl who had changed my life so easily even though we hadn't talked a lot. She had changed my life, bu she wasn't the only one. I wanted to share this feeling with Amy. No matter how much I had hated her at times, she had helped me realize that I had wings, she had helped me fly. She had transformed me to a beautiful dark angel. I had been beautiful; I had been amazing. But now my wings were gone, and being gay felt odd. It felt as though I had just discovered that I in reality was left-handed or just found out that Santa Clause isn't real. It was a little bizarre and hard to swallow.

Later that day, when I was packing up my books and basically getting ready to leave school, I was in the process of removing my phone from my back-pocket to the pocket in my jacket, when I once again remembered the text from Louisa. I didn't reckon it'd seem desperate if I replied to it now, so I held it in my hand for a few moments, before I clicked on the text she had sent me. I quickly typed, "Yay, I'm glad you also want to meet up :D What about tomorrow?" With this, I slipped the phone into my jacket pocket and walked out the door to the school grounds.

I ended up on that same bridge once again, and the water started flowing from my eyes. I was gay, I was gay and I knew it. And there was nothing I could do about it, nothing I could change. I was gay, but being gay didn't feel as natural as it had the other day on this very bridge. I didn't want to be gay.

My phone buzzed in my pocket. Somebody was calling me. In a vain hope that it was Louisa, I picked it up and answered the call. "'tis Emma," I said with a voice that was raw with emotions. I was hoarse from silence and crying, and I felt exhausted, overused. I was an old Kleenex somebody had squirted their snot all over. The person on the line did not introduce themselves.

"It's okay to be gay Emma," a gentle voice said in a calming way. I felt like I was being patted on the back, or receiving the biggest hug ever. Without even thinking over who it could be, I blurted out, "I'm gay Amy, I'm gay, and it's horrible and wrong, but also so right, and I'm just really tired of being a frigging lesbo already," I sobbed into the phone and fell to the ground, sobbing harder than ever as I sat on the ground on a bridge in a small town, salty tears flowing from my eyes and the nasal mucus running from my nose into my mouth. It was gross and so disgusting, all of it, my flowing snot and my tears, and the fact that I fucking was gay, and that Rochelle had been right, everything was just disgusting in that moment; except the voice on the line, soothing me, calming me down like a mother will do to a small child, telling me that it was okay, that she loved me, that everything was going to fit together, that everything was going to be okay, and I sobbed and sobbed, and everything was just too much.

I was gay, and I wasn't okay with it at all.

CHAPTER TWENTY FIVE

That night I couldn't fall asleep. I was afraid the nightmare would return, scarier than ever. Somewhere, deep down, I knew it wouldn't come back, when I had discovered my wings I had eliminated the nightmare forever, it was gone; but what if it wasn't? What if? All my life had been about all these 'what if's; I could never fully escape them. I spent the night imagining ways to come out – buying a pizza and arranging the pepperonis to spell 'I'm gay'; walking out of a closet; inviting my parents out to eat dinner and tell them there; shaving I'm gay into my hair (okay, maybe I didn't really consider that one); writing an email to the people I needed to come out to; tell them I had a really cool surprise, and take them to gay pride; all of it was ideas I had found while listening to the coming out stories earlier that afternoon. I wanted to come out, God, I wanted to come out so bad, but I was scared. I was horrified to be honest; what if my mom wouldn't accept me? What would my grandparents think of it? Would they think I'd be going to hell for thinking such impure thoughts about girls? What would people at school think? What did I even think of it? No, I knew what I myself thought of it. Being gay wasn't okay. Being a lesbian was disgusting; it was something no one should ever become.

I stayed up till the early hours of the morning, shaking with unshed tears and knowing that my entire day would be ruined from lack of sleep, but I couldn't help it. I just wanted to sob into my pillow, but I stayed strong. I had to be strong, prove that I could deal with being gay, deal with being a disgusting freak that never should've been born – at this point I was crying into my pillow and masking the racks of sobs running through my body ever so often by pressing the pillow against my mouth. I was gay, and I didn't want to be gay. I never wanted to feel this way, ever. I hadn't ever wanted to feel this terrible; I didn't understand what I had done to deserve this amount of pain. Slowly and steadily the sobs grew less frequent and I travelled to the worlds beyond ours; the world where being gay was okay, the worlds where you could go on adventures every day and never ever be bored. I travelled to the dream world.

*

I could've fallen asleep on my table at school in English class the following day, if it hadn't been for Mrs. LaCreepy's voice which had awoken me every time I dozed off my head in my arms lying on the table. My eyelids drooped down every other minute. I was so tired.

When finally we had a break between English and Physical Education I placed my head onto the table and tried to fall asleep. I say 'tried', because I definitely did not succeed. The thoughts raced around in my brain. How was I going to come out? How would people react? How was I ever going to be okay with being into chicks? But finally I dozed off, and wasn't awoken before I heard the bell signaling that the break was over. I hadn't packed any gym clothes I realized with an exasperated sigh, and started to walk out on the grounds towards the P.E. building. As I was walking, I realized one thing; the dark was truly gone. I hadn't been enveloped in darkness. I didn't know if I was relieved or not; I had become familiar with the dark, and I missed the wings. Not to mention the fact that the voice talking in the dark had been my dad's voice, my dad, whom I hadn't seen more than thrice a year for years and years on end.

I ran around after a feather-ball for two entire lessons, wearing my normal clothes, and I felt gross and sticky when I arrived back at the school for my lunch. I sat alone in the cafeteria, avoiding Rochelle as much as I possibly could. I didn't want to talk to her about the fact that I genuinely liked girls. I could feel her hurt gaze across the room, stabbing me in the back. I was a horrible person. I knew Rochelle had a really hard time right time, but yet I ignored her, and probably gave her more reasons to self-harm.

I couldn't do it though, I couldn't sit down beside her , Sophia and Lee, I just couldn't. I wanted to, but I couldn't do it. They'd notice there was something different about me, and they'd bug me about it until I gave in and told them everything. I sat there imagining how I'd tell them that I was so into girls that it wasn't even funny; I would tell them that I liked Louisa and their faces would be confused – but that was as far my imagination could carry me in one scenario; I did not know what they'd think of it. Perhaps Sophia would raise her eyebrows so much that her brows almost vanished in her locks of hair, her brown eyes confused, or maybe she'd scoot her chair away from me, disgusted. Lee would get angry, I imagined. He'd get up from his chair, screaming and throwing his hands in the air, calling me a freak, his brown eyes filled with hatred.

Or maybe he'd ask me if I'd be into a threesome. Rochelle's reaction was trickier to imagine. She was pansexual, and liked girls as well. But would she think it was disgusting to only like girls? Although I didn't like her like that, I couldn't bear the thought of losing my one true friend in this horrid high school.

I didn't know what they would think of me; that was all I knew. I had no idea. They could be warm, loving and accepting, but they could also be cold and hateful, spewing out words like 'freak', 'lesbo', or 'fag'. And that was the reason I couldn't sit with them. I just couldn't risk what little I had earned in my time here. I couldn't let them out me to the rest of the high school population.

Finally my lunch was over and done with, I had eaten every bite of the disgusting canteen food, and I could leave and go back to our classroom. In there I found a brown haired girl with a dimple in her left cheek sitting on my table. I sighed deeply, and walked towards her. Amy had bad timing; I definitely didn't want to talk to anybody right now. Finally I was standing in front of her – and suddenly the tears rushed down my cheeks.

"You're skipping class today," Amy said in a determined voice, and gripped my wrist tightly and dragged me out of the classroom.

I didn't resist her; all I did was to take my backpack on the way out, so I wouldn't have to return to the school, and we walked away from the scene. We just walked as I cried softly beside her. I didn't know where we were going, and I didn't know why; all I cared about was that we were walking there, and Amy took my hand, stroking the skin tenderly, lovingly. I loved this girl, I realized. She had become something like a best friend in a way nobody else ever had been; I loved her. Not in the way I loved Louisa, but nonetheless, I loved her.

We ended up in the place I would think of as 'our' place in many years to come – the harbor. She sat me down on the rock I'd sat on countless times now, and let me cry as she sat in front of me, soothingly grazing my cheek and holding my hand. She didn't say anything, she just let me cry, and slowly, steadily I stopped crying. The sobs grew fewer and fewer, and eventually everything fell silent.

We didn't even need to speak about what we were going to do; it just felt so painfully obvious. Amy enveloped my nose with her hand, and I placed my hands on my ears. I clenched my eyes shut and then it happened. The world around me disappeared.

Unlike the other times I had closed my eyes; I didn't find myself in darkness. I found myself bathed in light; light that was bright and white, clean somehow. It lit up everything, the light originating from nowhere. It just lit up everything. I looked back; I was standing up on my feet, the ground underneath them. There was dark behind me – but I knew that just was the black wings. I wasn't scared of them anymore.

Okay, that was a lie. I was more scared of them than I ever had been for the dark. Those wings were beautiful, but terrifying. I wanted to spread them out, fly like I had done once before, but I was so afraid of falling. I didn't want to hurt myself, so I just put up a wall and hid behind it.

I flapped my wings uselessly. I couldn't fly. I couldn't fly. And if I couldn't fly, what kind of angel was I?

Chapter Twenty Six

"I don't want those wings, you can have them," I sobbed in the moment my sea-blue eyes flew open. I screeched the words out, as the first sob racked throughout my entire body. I hid my head in my hands and mumbled, stumbling over the words as I murmured, just loud enough for Amy to hear, "You're the angel here, not me," I cradled myself back and forth, back and forth in an attempt to calm myself down. I needed to be calm. Amy sighed, and rested a soft, pale hand on my cheek. Her eyes were worried and slightly disappointed. She didn't say anything about my failure though;, she just sat there with her big eyes and brown hair, and looked so amazing. I couldn't believe I hadn't understood that she was an angel before now... "You know why this happened, don't you?" she asked me gently, after a little time had passed and I had calmed down, the tears still flowing softly down my cheeks.

"It's because... Now you've realized, er, something about yourself, but you haven't, eh, accepted it yet," she said hesitantly, stuttering a little every now and then. There was no doubt in my mind what she was talking about – she was talking about the fact that I knew I was a raging homosexual, but hated myself for being that. I sighed. "What is there to accept? I' m a freak," I murmured into my hands once again. "Hey," Amy said, and I felt he hand on my knee, and I looked up. She was smiling at me, a smile which calmed me down instantly. She looked like the synonym of a safe heaven. She looked so content and happy with herself, and even though I had failed, I couldn't help but feel that my spirit was a little higher now than a few seconds before.

"You've come far already Emma, you should remember to be proud of that," Amy said gently, continuing the sentence she had started moments before. I could feel the pride welling up in me.

She was right; I had come far already. I'd discovered my wings for Christ's sake! Now I just had to learn how to use them. Birds didn't just learn to fly in one day either. Rome wasn't built in a day, so why should I expect myself to build something up without it taking time? I smiled at Amy. "You know, you're really good at making people feel comfortable, once you've stopped pushing boundaries, or kiss people without liking them in that way," I said, hoping my remark would sting a little (I wasn't fully over how cruel she'd been to me, forcing me into the dark and all), but she just laughed and smiled at me. "That's right, I'm amazing at making people feel good baby," she said, chuckling lightly as she spoke. I continued smiling, as Amy got to her feet, kicking them around, as they clearly had fallen asleep while she had sat in front of me. When she had regained the feeling in her legs, she reached out a hand and dragged me up from the rock, placing me on my feet. "You're going home now," she said.

"I am?" I asked confused and a little annoyed. Why did she think it was fair to push me around? Amy just looked back at me and laughed. "Yup, and we're going to make a delicious sandwich with peanut butter and strawberry jelly," she said happily. I stared at the back of her head as she turned around again and dragged me after her. How did she know that sandwiches with peanut butter and jelly were one of my favorite things in the world? I had definitely never told her that. Maybe it was one of those angel things.

We passed Mrs. Smith's house on the way home. She was out in the garden and yelled a greeting as Amy dragged me past the perfectly watered begonias, and I yelled back, "Thanks for the other day, it helped me a lot!" before Amy had dragged me around the corner of a street, and Mrs. Smith was out of earshot. "Oi, I was talking to that lady!" I shouted at Amy. She smiled back at me, and my anger melted away. "We're going to eat delicious food, remember?" she exclaimed, and started running as we both saw my home. I ran after her, holding her hand loosely.

We made sandwiches, and they were exactly as delicious as I had imagined them. We sat down at the kitchen table with a plate in front of each of us. We were halfway through the sandwiches when I decided to bring out the big question; we hadn't spoken in a while, and were just looking at each other when I finally spoke up. "How come you know all this stuff about me? I mean, you knew I liked peanut butter and jelly on sandwiches, and you probably know other stuff too… How?" I asked, picking apart my sandwich, and stuffing my face with it.

"I'm a part of you Emma," she said gently, and placed a hand on mine. "I'm you, you're me," she whispered.

*

I managed to avoid Rochelle, Sophia and Lee for exactly three days and two boring math lessons, and the weekend was two of those days. They cornered me at the library where I was looking at How to Kill a Mockingbird, reading the preview on the back, when they arrived, each coming from a different direction, cornering me against the wall. I tried to shrug off how uncomfortable I felt; it was like standing in an elevator with a hundred strangers; it was that awkward to look into Sophia's amazing chocolate colored eyes on my right, Rochelle on my left, and Lee in front of me. They were staring me down. If looks could kill, I'd have died a thousand deaths in that moment.

"What the fuck do you think you're doing E?" Sophia said angrily. I was surprised she didn't grow claws; she was like an animal, a furious animal luring after its prey. I swallowed my spit. What was I going to do?

"Yeah, what do you think you're doing?" Lee asked, clearly taking the lead. "We've been so fucking worried; you don't even know how worried we've been. What are you doing, you haven't talked to us for days, and never replies to our text messages," I fiddled nervously with the hem of my shirt. I hadn't meant to hurt them, I just couldn't live with the fact that I was who I was, and I knew I'd mess up things if I told them the truth. The time I had spent with them had been so perfect, so much like a perfect dream world. I didn't want to lose that again, I wanted to preserve those beautiful, amazing memories. That was all it was – memories. I couldn't continue a friendship with them; it'd be too painful to hide who I was from them.

"I'm, I'm – I can't, I'm sorry, I just can't," I wept and pushed Sophia aside with a sob, and ran out of the room. I could hear them clattering behind me, but I didn't turn to look at them; I just ran and ran, ran and ran, ran out to the school grounds, where I sat down behind the P.E building, and cried my heart out for God knows what time that week. I felt so fucking weak, so overused, so… stupid. I was just a stupid girl with stupid sea-blue eyes and stupid brown hair that reached my stupid shoulders – I was so fucking stupid. I hated myself. I hated myself more than I ever had hated Annabelle for being my cousin and not just my friend; I hated myself more than I had ever hated Amy; I simply just hated myself, hated the world, hated everything. I didn't want to be gay, I didn't want to be bi, I didn't want to be anything at all; I didn't want to live anymore, I wanted to go buy some cocaine and snort it, just for the hell of it. It was supposed to feel amazing, and in that moment, I definitely didn't feel amazing. Rather, I felt like shit.

Slowly my tears stopped flowing, and I got to my feet, walked inside the school again – the break was over, and the students were all in class, so nobody saw my painfully obvious red face, which screamed out that I had cried. I walked to the bathroom, and cleaned myself up, placing a wet cloth on each of my eyes, to stop the light swelling. I sighed deeply as I sat down on the toilet with closed eyes, once again feeling the disappointment that I couldn't fly anymore. I had been able to once, but apparently not anymore. Not anymore. I sighed.

After about half an hour, I heard the bell ring, signaling that the lessons were over, and I got to my feet, washed my face yet again, and walked out of the toilet, my legs quivering like crazy. I felt so very tired and worn-out. I didn't want to face Rochelle in my math class, but I had to deal with it sooner or later. I had to suck it up, be tough and strong; fight the battle. I had to take it like a man. I found my iPod and listened to the most fitting song I could think of at the moment – a song from an old Disney movie. "Make a Man Out Of You." That was what I needed. I needed to suck it up, be a man and stop whining like a little bitch. I couldn't be sat moping around all day, just because I was gay and didn't want to be.

I walked out in the corridor, which was now packed with students talking and chattering away, sitting on the tables, leaning against the walls, or just standing in the middle of the hall with their books pressed against their chests.

Even though there were loads of people, I felt very lonely.

CHAPTER TWENTY SEVEN

I tried to keep avoiding Lee, Sophia and Rochelle, but they weren't having any of it. Rochelle switched seats with the girl I sat next to in math class, a girl everyone called by her last name; Adams, Sophia was sitting all the way at the back of the class, and Lee's stare was piercing the back of my head. In a strange way, I was quite relieved that they were so determined to stay friends with me. I wasn't used to people wanting to be my friend – I had always just had Annabelle, and don't get me wrong, Annabelle was amazing, and I loved her, but she was three years younger, and sometimes you just needed people to get you fully and wholly. These guys got me. They understood me. They loved me. Why else would they be so intent to get me back on track with them? But then again, I couldn't help but get a little annoyed. Hadn't I told them that I couldn't explain what was going on? I had a lot of mixed feelings.

Rochelle slid notes to me every other moment. Basically they all read what she was going to do to my body once she'd gotten hold of me. My favorite one was the note that read that she'd cut me into pieces with a fork and dump me in the river. I started laughing when she sent me that one, and earned a detention for it, but I didn't care. I couldn't really be bothered to care – it was nice to be wanted, although I couldn't return the favor.

But there were other, more pressuring issues than Rochelle, Lee Adams and Sophia Lexington to think about. I could definitely feel that I had been absent in quite a few lessons, and I knew it would show on my average grades, and make them very-much-less-than-average if I wasn't careful. I had to work harder, but it was so difficult with the thoughts flying around in my head, buzzing like bees; I couldn't get a single moment to recollect my thoughts and actually do something about the issue. It was just that - an issue; even though I was smart, (well, I was smarter than a three year old, that was at least something) I couldn't catch up with all the homework in just a few hours, and have a decent result, and coincidentally that was all the time I had to finish my math homework. A few hours. I scribbled down the answers, not caring that my handwriting was frantic and hard to read. It would be a horrible piece of work anyway. I spent the English lesson ignoring Mrs. LaCreepy and her boney hands around the piece of chalk making eerie noises against the blackboard. I completely ignored her, and worked on the math questions. Half of them I didn't know what to do. Perhaps I wasn't smarter than a three year old when it came down to it.

Rochelle continuously sent me notes throughout the lesson, and I tried to ignore them and focus on the important things (okay, maybe my math homework wasn't really important, but it was fucking necessary, and that was almost the same thing,) but it was difficult. I couldn't help chortling at the ridiculous threats she sent me ("I'm going to cut off your ears and stuff your head with candy so small kids will hit you to get it out," or "I'm going to sit on your leg until you can't feel it anymore," was a few other of my favorites) and every time I did that, I saw Rochelle lean satisfied back in her chair. I wondered if that had been her plan all along, distracting me from the thoughts that buzzed around in my head. My mind was like a cube of bees. They were buzzing around in there, the thoughts of where Amy was now, and how I was going to explain to everyone that I liked girls, and how people would react, and I really wished Amy had been there, right there, sitting beside me instead of that girl called Adams, which I didn't know at all. But she wasn't. She'd always been there when I needed her, so I didn't understand why she wasn't here now.

Sure, she had scared the hell out of me by appearing in strange places, but she'd just tried to help me. And she had helped me, a lot actually. I didn't know how I ever could repay that debt.

I needed to pee. Ugh. I sighed and raised my hand, closing my math book. "What, Oaksby?" LaCreepy said with a tired voice; she couldn't have avoided noticing how I hadn't been paying attention at all.

"Can I have a lavatory pass?" I asked and batted with my eyes, trying to seem as innocent as possible. It wasn't like I was going to leave the school, but LaCreepy was so intimidating that I felt like I had to be pure and innocent. She sighed and nodded tiredly, before she turned around and continued writing on the blackboard. I got to my feet, and tiptoed out of the room, with everyone's' gaze at my back. I walked out to the toilet, shut the door, sat down and started doing my business.

And suddenly – it came as quite a surprise – Amy was standing in the room. The door didn't open or close behind her (and how would she even open the door since it was locked?!); suddenly she just… was there. I yelled out in surprise, but next thing I knew, she was covering my mouth. "Hush," she whispered, and I fell silent. Of all the places I'd seen Amy – my bedroom, in the classroom of this school, in the room where we had biology, and last, but not least, the harbor – of all those places, this was the strangest of them all. I was on the toilet for Christ sake man; couldn't I expect at least a little privacy?! She smiled gently at me, and slowly removed her hand. I took a deep inhalation of nice, clean air, and exhaled slowly.

"What are you doing here?" I asked hesitantly; Amy wouldn't just show up without a reason. It was nice to see her again; I could feel my entire body relaxing as though I had just stepped into a hot bathtub filled with water and soap. Amy smiled; a soft, beautiful, genuine smile. I smiled back. She shook her head as though she couldn't believe me, and said, "Isn't that obvious Emma Oaksby?" Okay, right now, I couldn't help hating her a little. She acted as though she was the clever adult, and I just was a stupid baby. "No, actually it isn't. Not to me," I said annoyed, and felt my mouth pucker slightly in anger.

She sighed, and leaned herself against the wall. "Well, I'm here to help you accept yourself," she explained with a voice as though telling somebody they're on their deathbed; she sounded concerned and worried. I didn't understand why, and shook my head hesitantly. "I- I don't understand," I said with a quivering voice. I could feel my lips tremble, and my entire body was shaking. Accept myself? There was only one thing I needed to accept, only one thing I hadn't yet embraced… my sexuality. I sat on my hands, trying to avoid letting myself getting to the point where I'd hit a wall or something. I wanted to break something, and I wished there was something made of glass in here; I would have loved to smash it against the wall.

"I think you understand," Amy whispered gently. It was so quiet you could have heard a pin drop to the floor. I nodded, and hid my head in my hands that restlessly pulled at my hair, as I tried to regain feeling of them after I'd sat on them. I needed to embrace who I was.

"I know you're getting lost in the amount of your homework, so I'm not going to help you right now. Now you shall go back to your lesson with the lovely Mrs. LaCreevy, and then I'll meet you at the entrance when schools finished," she said with a definitive tone in her voice. I got to my feet and unlocked the door. She reached out a hand, and I, slightly confused, shook it. She smiled at me and said, "I'll see you later then," and then – then… then she was gone. Poof; just like that. But in the brief second before she left, I was sure I saw something… I shook my head in disbelief when I was left alone in the crappy school toilet. It couldn't be.

But I was pretty sure that I had seen a pair of golden wings spreading behind Amy's back.

I left the washroom and returned to my class. I continued working on my homework, with just as many (if not more), thoughts than before I had entered that bathroom. So I was supposed to just… accept that I was gay? Keep dreaming baby; there was no way I ever could love the fact that I loved girls. It was disgusting, it was wrong. But I couldn't change it. Perhaps it really was best to learn to get over this fear? I sighed, and continued scribbling at my math homework. I would find out what I was supposed to do with my sexuality when I met Amy later today.

Chapter Twenty Eight

When school was over, I walked to the entrance of the school. I was nervous, although I didn't know why. Amy was there, waiting for me, leaning against the boring, grey brick wall. I sighed as I reached her. Her face lit up in a sweet smile, and reached out a hand for me to take, so we wouldn't lose each other in the crowd of students leaving the school. Once again I got that feeling of freedom that not even the fourth of July could've ever given me. I smiled at her. She was just trying to help me; clumsily yes, but she was just trying to help me. And I couldn't help but be grateful for that. She'd shown me my beautiful wings, and she was teaching me how to fly.

This thought reminded me of something. "Amy, do you have wings?" I asked nervously, biting my lip as she dragged me out onto the streets surrounding the school. She didn't reply, and that was enough answer for me. I followed her, careful to step on each stub of cigarette I saw on the street, remembering the first night I met her. I had cried afterwards, although I didn't want to. I didn't want to be a weak girl; I wanted to be strong and beautiful, a fighter. I wasn't any of those things. I was weak, I was stupid, I was ugly, and apparently I was also gay. I didn't want to be either of those things. She dragged me down the streets as I was consumed in my thoughts of how horrible a person I was. Because of this, I didn't notice where we were going, before we were standing in front of a house. I didn't know where I had expected her to bring me, perhaps the harbor which kind of was "our" place now, or perhaps to my home; but that wasn't where she led me. I was standing in front of a house built of red bricks: Louisa's house. The door opened before I even closed the gate, and Louisa was standing at the doorstep wearing a pair of worn-out slippers, looking me dead in the eyes and smiling widely at me..

We ran towards each other, running and running, her from the door and out on the street, and me towards the door; and suddenly we were hugging and swaying back and forth, cradling each other tightly, and the next thing I knew, our faces were inches from each other, and I looked into her beautiful grey and blue eyes. She was so beautiful, so amazing. "Can I kiss you?" she whispered gently as she tucked a loose strand of brown hair back behind my ear. I nodded faintly, inhaling her smell as she leaned even closer, and as her lips touched mine, I could only think of one thing – that she had asked for permission, that she had waited for me to consent this time, and I thought she was perfect. She was perfect for me.

I sensed Amy standing beside me, but when I came up for air, she wasn't there. I didn't mind. She'd given me a gift; she'd given me Louisa. I loved Louisa; it seemed so clear and logical now. I was gay, and I was in love. I was in love with an amazing girl, who, it seemed, loved me back. As our lips parted, she took my hand and I followed her into the house. She led me through the house, once again pointing to each door telling me what room it was, and I smiled. I could feel the tears well up in my eyes. Not because I was sad, not even because I was happy; it was because I was fully and wholly euphoric. I had realized who I was, I had accepted it now, and the best part was that I had found somebody else who did. She accepted me completely as I was.

I may be stupid, I may be ugly, I might even be weak; but I'm proud of it. I am who I am; a weak, stupid, ugly, gay girl; a frigging weird lesbo, and I'm fucking awesome. I deserve to love myself.

*

I left Louisa's house a few hours later; we had been making out on her bed, her hands around my waist, and my sweaty, nervous hands running through her hair. She'd been lying on top of me, and it had been wonderful and beautiful. I could go on describing how we had kissed and how her lips tasted of strawberry lip-gloss, but that could take up multiple pages, and I want to tell this story and not the tale of Louisa Smith's soft, gentle lips.

So I left, around six pm, as I had to get home for dinner, and talk to my mom about how I hadn't even told I was going out. I really looked forward to that, I thought sarcastically.

When I entered the house, I heard a crash and a voice cussing, yelling at me for startling them. It was my mom; she had dropped a plate. She decided to blame me for it, bringing it up multiple times through dinner, when she wasn't roasting me for news about what I had been doing, as I hadn't come straight home. Hah, 'straight' home – get it? Because I'm not straight, even though she thinks I am?

We were cleaning up the kitchen when I felt it. A voice in my head; not the voice from the dark – this was a warm, nice voice, a gentle voice. It said, "Meet me outside," and then my head fell silent. I didn't have to think twice about whom it was – it was obvious to me. It had been Amy. I was definitely doing as she said; it had never harmed me to follow her advice.

"I know I came home quite late today, but I have to go out again," I said nervously, as I cleaned the last pot and handed it to her.

"You're not going out again, young lady. You've already been out 'till late,"

"I have to meet my helper," I said, watching her reaction.

She froze completely, her entire stature just froze, and she stared at me. "Your... your helper? Well then... You're allowed to go out. But be back at nine o'clock," she said, and continued to dry the pot with the cloth in her hands. I could see her hand shake.

So with my mom's blessing I left the house and met Amy on the corner of the block. She took my hand and dragged me onto the streets in that impatient way that only she could pull off without me getting sick of it. I told her to stop for a moment, and we stood still on the street for a second or two, for I had an eerie feeling in the nape of my neck; like somebody was watching me.

I just brushed off the feeling; but if I had looked back at the window of my house I would have noticed a lady standing there, watching me closely.

The million dollar question: where did Amy bring me? If you answered "the harbor", you were damn right. If you didn't answer that, well, that sucks for you. Lost a million bucks, huh? Joke aside; Amy brought me to the harbor and sat me down on the "usual" rock. She sat down in front of me, looking up at me, sitting on her knees. Once again I was reminded how that posture had to hurt, but she did it for me. She took my hand and let her thumb stroke it delicately.

"This is the last time you'll see me," she said soothingly, and stroke my hand. "But I'll always be there, in here," she continued, now whispering intimately, and put her other hand over her heart. I could feel the tears starting to roll down my face. No matter how much I sometimes had hated Amy, I had taken a liking to her in the end. I couldn't bear the thought of never seeing her again, never holding her hand and feeling so free again; I wanted to be friends with her forever. At the same time, I knew she was right. It was time for her to return to her true home. She smiled at me, showing off the dimple in her cheek that reminded me so much of Louisa, and the crooked teeth that really could use a set of braces sparkled to me from her rosy lips. I leaned over and pecked her lips softly; not the kind of kiss you'd give a lover – it was a kiss to say thank you. I was so very grateful for everything she had taught me in the last few weeks.

"Can I see your wings?" I asked with a trembling voice, "- just this once? Please?" I pleaded, the next tears spilling out of my eyes and covering my face. Amy smiled at me; I could see she was getting teary as well. "It's been fun to help you Emma," she said, and stroke my hand once again, before she got to her feet and said, "I'll let you see them, but don't ever tell anybody you saw them," obviously referring to my question about her wings.

Slowly, something rose on her back; something grew out of it, like a flower blooming. It only took a few seconds before the wings were spread out. They weren't black like mine – no, they were gold, shining and sparkling like gold. I reached out a hand, and touched the soft feathers that so very much resembled mine in softness and beauty. I smiled softly, as I gently played with a feather. "Can I have one?" I asked childishly. Amy smiled at me, but shook her head. She leaned forwards and hugged me tenderly. A soft, warm hug, which withheld all the emotions we had for each other. Her golden wings spread behind her, and she pulled away from our affectionate hug. She waved lightly at me, and smirked through her tears; for her eyes were flooding with big, wet tears.

And then she was gone.

Chapter Twenty Nine

The next morning, mom was acting weird. She sat still at the breakfast table, and picking at the toast on her plate, her appetite apparently gone. I didn't want to ask her; I'd probably just get a lecture on how people sometimes wanted to be left alone and sometimes wanted to talk, and be told off for not knowing what she wanted. I picked at my sandwich with ham and cheese. I felt so lost without Amy. I had ended up depending on her help, needing it like a boy needs his mother's side. Where was she now? Up in heaven? Was she an angel? Was that why her wings were golden? She had been so... so... beautiful as she said goodbye... Her wings had stretched themselves behind her and she had flown away, with her wings flapping back and forth, or at least I thought that was what happened. I couldn't really remember...

I broke off a piece of bread from my sandwich (I didn't want to eat cereal) and threw it into my open mouth. This would usually tick off my mom; she hated when I didn't behave like the young lady I was (or rather; the young lady she wanted me to be), but she just sighed deeply and picked at her food once again. She looked so old once again, and I felt an urge to hug her tightly. I didn't do it though, it would feel too strange. We rarely ever hugged anymore.

Finally she spoke up. She looked at me, a glare that seemed so... disappointed, so lost, so misunderstanding. I raised my eyebrows lightly as if to say, "spit it out," and she opened her mouth. The next words weren't what I had expected... at all.

"Did you really meet your helper yesterday? You didn't just go out with a couple friends?" she asked, her lips quivering like a baby on the verge of crying. I cocked my eyebrows again. "Uh, of course I met my helper - do you think I'm lying or something?" I asked, for some reason I couldn't help but feel nervous. Amy had been supposed to be a girl, perhaps Mrs. Smith had told her that she was, in fact, a girl?

"Then how do you explain that I saw you leaving with a girl and not a boy?" she asked, her voice almost hateful. She was angry, but moreover, she was afraid. Anger always comes from fear, in most cases anyway. She was afraid of the person I might be.

"She was my helper mom," I said, trying to avoid letting my voice quiver. I felt so fragile and delicate, like something made of glass, I was made out of glass, and I'd crash to the floor, broken.

"No she wasn't. You're not gay," she said, brushing off my confession. I could feel the tears stinging in my eyes. I got to my feet and ran to my room, slamming the door after me, hearing a loud, satisfying bang, before I found the key and locked the door. She wouldn't find the spare key for at least an hour or so; we had no idea where our spare keys were. Mom shouted something about my bad manners and how she had given up on me. It stung, it really did, but it also felt odd, like I wasn't really in the room. Like I was watching it all on a screen, it felt like that. It was strange. I could sit there, against the door. My thoughts weren't at all foggy as they often had been lately what with fighting the dark. It's time parents starts to teach children how to love, not what to love, I thought, as a tear glided down my cheek, and I angrily brushed it away.

I wanted Amy's arms around me so badly, or even better, Louisa's lips to calm me down, touching my skin softly and gently, her hands touching my skin caringly, caressing my cheekbones and playing with my hair. I smiled vaguely. I missed her; I could feel that in every ounce of my body. I needed to see her.

I sat down on the bed and sighed deeply. It felt nice to sit there, inhaling and exhaling, inhaling and exhaling slowly, slowly, as I felt the tears roll from my eyes, getting stuck in my eyelashes for the briefest of seconds before they continued to roll down my cheeks.

Once again I started to wonder where Amy was now. Out helping some other kid? Was she in Heaven, flying around other angels playing at a harp? I chortled. Amy and playing harp did not seem to be words that fit together in the same sentence. It just didn't seem like her. Amy was a badass motherfucker (not in the literal term) and I couldn't help but imagine she stirred up loads of trouble in Heaven. She probably set fire to everything because the flames looked so beautiful. But who had she even been? I wasn't sure. Was she an angel? What was Amy – or rather; who had Amy been? I wondered on the subject, as I chewed on a root of a nail. And then – the answer came to be in a surge of inspiration. I stumbled through the room, sat down in front of the computer, opening a new tab, and quickly typed: translate, in the search bar. I clicked onto the first translating device that showed up onto the page. I clicked on the options, and soon enough the screen said, English > Latin. Sexuality, I typed, my heart beating fast, and waited for a few seconds for my slow computer to come up with the answer. And there it was: Sexualitatis.

Amy was – or had been, before she left - Sexualitatis. She had been my sexuality. I placed a hand on my heart, remembering what she had said. "I'll always be there, in here." No, Amy hadn't left. She still lived in my heart, lived in me, in every heartbeat she was with me. "Thanks Amy," I whispered, and felt my heart beating slowly. And somehow I knew that she heard me.

Chapter Thirty

I was walking to the post office by myself on my way home from school. All alone; I was going to get the package I had bought online. Something that would scream 'gay' with big neon letters – or at least I hoped it would. A few days had passed, and mom had calmed down, although she still thought I lied about Amy being my Helper. I hated this kind of thing; being mistrusted when you're actually telling the truth.

So that day, a rainy Friday afternoon I was walking on the streets towards the post office to retrieve my treat, my little gift to myself; a box of rainbow bracelets.

When I finally had my grip on the box the bracelets were sent within, I couldn't help but shed a couple of tears. This just meant so much to me; I was able to get a gay accessory; and if that wasn't cool I didn't know what was.

As I walked home, opening the package as I walked, taking on the two bracelets, I decided to celebrate it. I needed to let go of all my worries.

And how would I celebrate it, you ask?

…by coming out.

*

"Mom, I have to show you something," I said as I nervously chewed on a piece of spearmint gum. She looked mildly surprised, but nodded and got up from the couch and turned the television off. "Yeah, sure, I'm coming now," she said calmly, and followed me out of the living room. With shaky legs I walked up the stairs until we reached my room. "Wait here, I'll call when I'm ready for you to step in," I said, my voice trembling hard. I was scared; beyond that even. I was horrified. She nodded once again, and I walked into the room, closing the door after me, before I ran to my drawer. I quickly withdrew the rainbow bracelets I had ordered from Amazon and walked to my closet, which I stepped into.

"You can come in now," I shouted, and closed the door to the closet. It was dark, but it didn't scare me the slightest. I had experienced the kind of dark that swallowed everything; this was nothing. I could hear her enter the room, and imagined her looking around, confused over where I was hiding... I could hear her shoes clicking impatiently against the floor. Her expensive Jimmy Choos, I expected.

I clutched onto my rainbow bracelets for dear life, as if my life depended on it. Maybe my life really depended on it. What if she didn't accept me? What if her love was too much to ask for?

No, it wasn't too much to ask for. I knew that they – 'them' being my mom and the rest of society - had to accept me if they had any decency, but what if they didn't? What if I got kicked out of the house? What if she was going to hate me? And what about my dad? I rarely ever saw him, what if he'd hate me for who I was? He had been the voice in my nightmares, I didn't want him to be my nightmares come alive – I didn't want them to hate me.

They can't hate me, please, I want their love and their acceptance, I thought desperately and pressed my nails against my palm, trying to calm myself down. Pain always helped on the buzzing thoughts in my head; I could understand why Rochelle would cut to feel herself.

"Hi mom," I said nervously, and pushed the door open.

"I'm a lesbian," I said. And with those words I stepped out of the closet.

EPILOGUE

And to this day, I'm still learning how to love and accept myself fully and wholly. It's a hard task; pride is not an easy thing to obtain, it's challenging; but once you've learnt to love yourself as you are, you'll find that you really aren't that much different from everyone else. You may enjoy skating like me, you may not. You may be very feminine, you may be very masculine, you may be a mix, or you may not really be either. And that's okay. Because what matters, isn't your parts; what matters is what's inside your heart.

To this day, I'm still gay. And to this day, I hope you'll understand that living your life as you want it to be lived will give you more happiness than hide in the closet. I hope you'll break out of the cage you've been trapped in for so long. Always, always be yourself. It will give you less pain in the end. Stretch out those beautiful, dark wings and fly. Fly towards the sunset – follow the rainbows you see, direct your course after the stars. They'll lead you to your destiny.

CPSIA information can be obtained at www.ICGtesting.com
Printed in the USA
BVOW08s0840051016

464215BV00001B/32/P